REMOTE FEED

DAVID GILBERT

SCRIBNER

SCRIBNER
1230 Avenue of the Americas
New York, NY 10020

Designed by Brooke Zimmer
Set in Sabon
Manufactured in the United States of America

1 3 5 7 9 10 8 6 4 2

Library of Congress Cataloging-in-Publication Data

Gilbert, David, 1967–
Remote feed / David Gilbert.
p. cm.
Contents: Cool moss—Remote feed—Anaconda wrap—
Don't go in the basement—Graffiti—Opening day—Girl with large
foot jumping rope—CPR—At the Déjà Vu—Still in motion.
I. Title
PS3557.I383R46   1998
813'.54—dc21   97-42234
CIP

ISBN 0-684-84306-4

"Remote Feed" originally appeared in Harper's Magazine, "Graffiti" in The New Yorker, "Cool Moss" in altered form in the Mississippi Review and in New Stories of the South, Best of 1996, and "Girl with Large Foot Jumping Rope" in altered form in Cutbank magazine.

For my mother and father

Contents

Cool Moss

I T WAS the summer of theme parties. The Millers started it in June with line dancing. They'd found some group from Texas who called themselves Get In Line! and we watched and followed these sequined wonders as they stomped through the "Achy-Breaky" and the "Mason-Dixon." The Bissels tried to top the Millers a few weeks later with a psychic named Francine. She read palms, tarot cards, was even able to talk to Lena Bissel's great-grandfather, but like so many spiritualists she had no sense of humor and did not appreciate Chuck Hubert's zombie walk. Soon after that the Makendricks transformed their annual July Fourth party into what would have been a spectacular kite party had there been any wind. Laura Makendrick broke into very public tears. And eventually Zoe and I made a stab at it. We concocted a "Foods of the World" party which quickly turned into a "Drinks of the World" party. Once again Charlie Hubert performed his zombie walk—a few people always egg him on—and a table was broken, certainly no antique. I really don't know what it was about that summer, maybe we were all just restless, but normal parties felt dull and forgetful. Instead, there had to be a something learned even if it was that borscht does in fact taste like shit and a healthy supply of rum can save almost any party.

Tonight belonged to the Greers, Bill and Tammy. In the inferno of our friends they dwell in the third circle: the friends of friends with money. Lots of money. I sat downstairs on the couch and waited for Zoe. We were running late but I didn't care. An awful rumor had spread that there would be no alcohol served, something about false courage and a numbing of the brain. Yes, I thought, booze will do that to you. Thank God. So I was having a drink which quickly turned into a series of drinks, all lit with gin. That summer I was drinking gin. But I wasn't smoking.

The television was on and my three-year-old son was propped a few feet from the screen. Static raised his fine blond hair. The beginning of *Chitty Chitty Bang Bang* was playing on the VCR. Ray loved it. I knew because he had his hands jammed down his elastic pants and he mumbled about cars—"Vroom, Vroom"—as he squeezed his groin like a toy horn. In May he had discovered the first joy of the pleasure principle. We tried to thwart this habit by continually slapping him on the wrist and looking angry and pointing a finger to the ever-watchful sky, but he still carried on, our little boner boy. And nowhere was off limits. Restaurants. Birthday parties. He could pin the tail on the donkey with one hand. For a while we considered building a cardboard skirt, like the kind that prevents a dog from scratching his recently pinned ears, at least that's the joke we told gullible friends.

"He'll grow into it," I said to the nervous baby-sitter. She was sitting on the edge of a chair, a knapsack hugging her shoulders. Her name was Gwen and she had a large head and a large nose. I wondered if the kids at school were merciless toward her. Sombrero face.

She giggled. I thought of following up with a gag about Dick Van Dyke, but I wasn't sure if she'd even know who Dick Van Dyke was and I didn't want her to just hear the words "dick" and "dyke." So I offered her a soft drink instead.

"No thanks, I'm fine." She also had a bad complexion. I figured baby-sitting was a relief to her on Saturday nights.

"We won't be late," I told her.

"That's all right. I mean, it doesn't matter." She shrugged her knapsack. "I have lots of work." And she smiled without showing her teeth. I thought the worse: braces and receding gums.

"And he's easy," I said, gesturing toward my boy. "After this, another video, and if he's still awake after that, pop in another." I went over to the folding table that acts as our bar and mixed myself another drink. "He's seen them all a hundred times, the same damn movies, over and over again, but still, you know." My point clinked out in falling ice, and there was silence except for Truly Scrumptious singing her song. I sat back down. On the floor above I could hear Zoe's maneuverings. I didn't want to rush her; she was always feeling rushed. It was better to stay quiet than to bitch about being late. Just accept the situation. And I had that familiar feeling of waiting in an airport lounge for a delayed plane, and the more I waited the more I became convinced that this plane would crash over Ohio or skid into the ocean and that this drink would be my last drink and that this moment would be my last memory of things.

Soon Zoe came downstairs and I was relieved to see her. She gave me an expression of exasperation. "Sorry," she said.

"No problem." I lifted my glass to show her that I had been taking advantage of the lag time.

She said to the baby-sitter, "You must be Gwen."

The baby-sitter stood up. "Yes, hello Mrs. Scott."

"Well." Zoe's hands dropped to her side and she took a deep breath. She was beautiful, tanned from the summer, firm from jogging, and her hair had recovered some of its youthful blondness. "Just put him to bed when he gets tired. He's had dinner but if he gets hungry, give him a fruit roll-up. They're in the cupboard." I used to love to watch Zoe think. Her deep-set eyes have these attractive pouches and when she thinks she seems to search them for misplaced items. "Oh, and the Greers' phone number is by the kitchen phone, along with the emergency numbers."

The baby-sitter was nodding her huge head. "Got it," she said.

Zoe turned to me. "Okay, we're off." She walked over to Ray and slumped her knees against his back. "Ray, we're going," she said in a louder voice.

"Yep."

"We'll be back in just a little bit." I knew that Zoe wanted a child that would cry at such departures and wrap helpless arms around her and wail terribly. But Ray just sat there, hands down his pants, readying himself for a stupid car that could fly.

I ruffled his hair and said, "Have a good time." And as Zoe went toward the front door, I topped off my drink and took it with me. "'Bye now," I said, a bit awkwardly.

THE GREERS live just far enough away to remind us that we don't live in the truly nice neighborhood. "You know they're not serving any booze," I said.

"Yes."

"They've got more money than anyone and they're not serving booze. That just doesn't seem right. There's no heavy machinery involved." Zoe was quiet and looked like a weight lifter before attempting a clean and jerk. "You all right?" I asked.

"I'm not in the mood for a party tonight," she said.

"I hear you. Especially a party without booze." The sky had this grenadine glow. Months earlier a volcano had erupted on some distant island in the Philippines. A whole village was destroyed, fifty-seven people burned up and blown into the atmosphere—a definite tragedy—but all that summer every sunset seemed straight out of Hollywood.

"They have a surprise in store." Zoe pushed down the visor and checked her makeup in the pop-up vanity mirror. She wiped at the corners of her mouth. "I hate surprises," she said.

"Me too." And as we passed under tree-lined streets, I knew that there were eyes on the two of us and that we were somehow talking to those eyes, a third-party viewer, a witness, a ghost. "Surprises are for suckers," I said. The houses and front lawns grew progressively bigger. I rolled down the window so that the rushing air could enter our conversation.

"Malachi?"

"What?"

She paused for a second. I thought she was going to say something that would force me to pull the car over and face her. A hearty dialogue. But there wasn't any melodrama in our life—no affairs, no unemployment problems, no addictions—and we still thought that people on daytime talk shows were freaks. We were simply bored.

"What?" I said again.

Zoe reached over and clicked on the radio. The volume was too high but neither one of us bothered to turn it down. And I didn't drive any faster, just a flat thirty-five miles per hour.

THE GREERS' driveway was filled with cars and edged with standing torches. We parked on the street along with a few other late arrivals and followed the bending line of torches to the house: a large neocolonial, white with black shutters. During Christmas they placed an electric candle in each window. It was quite dramatic. And during Easter they hosted a huge Easter-egg hunt. They put a hundred bucks in the big egg. Kids would sprint and dive into bushes. But Ray was hopeless, sitting down and devouring the first chocolate bunny he came across.

"How do I look?" Zoe asked me.

"Fine."

"Really?"

"Yes."

From behind the house we heard a noise. It wasn't a social noise, a mingling of chitchat, music, and laughter; it was more like an angry swarm of mosquitoes, or, worse yet, a solitary two-hundred-and-fifty-pound mosquito. Mosquito-man. My mind tripped onto a late-night movie I had recently seen—*The Island of Dr. Moreau*—and I remembered those failed genetic experiments. Boar-man. Weasel-man. Orangutan-man. They terrorized a bare-chested Michael York. And at two in the morning I rooted for them to rip his body into pretty blond shreds.

"Take my hand," I said to Zoe.

We circled around some bushes, a bit of mulch, a bird-bath, and then walked through a gate which opened onto a beautiful back lawn—almost an acre and a half of perfect Bermuda grass. Off to the side, huddled in a circle, our group of friends hummed with their heads lowered, their arms intertwined. Just behind them a fifteen-foot stretch of coals glowed hot. It looked like a strange pep rally.

"Are we playing State tomorrow?" I whispered.

"Maybe it's a barbecue."

We stood still and no one noticed us. No one said, "Hey, it's the Scotts." No one offered us drinks or cheese puffs. No one cared. The circle was closed, and we didn't want to be one of those pushy couples. Besides, we were late, we didn't have any party rights. So we just watched as the hum slowly grew around them. A neighbor's dog howled, its timbre much more profound. And soon the hum reached a breathless pitch, and faces and arms slowly lifted toward the sky as if these people were chanting refugees waiting for the helicopters to drop down supplies from L. L. Bean. Finally, the hum ended with a lung-emptying "*Ahhh*," and there was cheering and smiling and one man, a tall guy in a shiny suit, said, "Did you feel the power?" Everyone nodded. "Yes?" he asked. He glanced around the group. "Well, that's the power of positive thinking." He made a point of training his eyes on each and every person. "That's the power you hold trapped within your body." He fisted his hands. "The power you never let out." Raised his finger. "Why?" Paused. "Because of fear."

Still no one noticed us. Attention was focused on this man. He had a manufactured face, smooth and with only a few lines to delineate a mouth, a nose, eyes. His voice was a personal whisper spoken to a crowd. I was sure he had a set of self-help videos in the trunk of his car, maybe an infomercial in the works. "Fear," he continued, "is what we have to overcome. Most of us are still children. We are afraid of the dark, afraid of the unknown, afraid to succeed. Why? Because if we try to succeed, if we put ourselves on the line, we can fail." I tried to catch the eyes of a few friends by making quick faces, but no eyebrows raised in recognition.

"Maybe these are the Stepford friends," I said to my wife.

"Huh?"

"You know, Robot people."

"Shhh."

"Now." The man clapped his hands. "I see some new guests have arrived." He gestured toward us like a game-show host displaying a brand-new washer and dryer. "So I think it's a good time for a break. But remember, let's psych each other up. We're part of a team." And then, with surprising quickness, he left the group and came over to us. "Hi," he said. "I'm Robert Porterhouse."

"I'm Zoe Scott, and this is my husband Mal."

We shook hands. He had a pinky ring and I hate pinky rings. He also had an expensive gold watch that hung loosely from his wrist.

"Well, are the two of you ready?" he asked.

"For what?" I said.

He grasped our forearms. "To change your life. To become who you want to be."

I smiled. "A baseball player? Sure."

I could tell by the way Zoe looked at me that she wanted to hit me on the arm, but instead she quickly pushed her voice over mine. "Why not," she said. I was a little put off by her enthusiasm. We used to laugh at our born-again friends.

"Great, Zoe. You have to align your belief system so that you get what you want."

"Even if it's a bigger house? A Porsche," I said.

"Sure, if that's what you want."

"How eighties," I said.

"No Mal, it's about what you want." He poked the air in front of my chest. "About what's in here." He glanced over our shoulders. "Now, I've got to check on things. I'll see you in a few." And he walked away.

I turned to Zoe. "And that night, Malachi Scott learned how to live."

"Don't be such a cynic."

I grabbed Zoe by the arms. "Did they get to you too?" I made a plea to the heavens. "You bastards!"

"Jesus, how drunk are you?"

"Not enough for this crap."

"You're going to make a great bitter old man."

"It's the gin. But thanks anyway."

Zoe was once a fan of my banter, thinking it was smart and urbane and very round-table, but now she turned away and made a disparaging sigh. "So clever," she said.

The circle had broken up and smaller groups formed. Bill and Tammy Greer saw us and waved and came over. Nervous enthusiasm creased their athletic faces. He was of Norwegian descent. She was of Finnish descent. They both wore the same shade of blue.

"Hey, you guys," Tammy said.

We apologized for being late, then I gave Tammy a kiss, and Zoe gave Bill a kiss, and Tammy gave Zoe a kiss, and Bill shook my hand. After that, we had little to say.

"So," I said. "What's going on here? A barbecue? A little luau?" I swung my hips.

"No, no," Bill said, shaking his head. "Something a lot more . . . powerful."

"Okay," I said. "Powerful."

"Yep." Bill turned toward the burning coals. A man in asbestos boots was spreading them with a long metal rake. "We're going to walk across those coals." He spoke like a man with a crazy dream.

Tammy curled her arm around Bill and gave him a squeeze. They were terminally in love: if one died, the other would soon follow. "And we'll never be the same," she said.

"That's what I've gathered," I said.

Bill gave us a spirited thumbs-up sign. "And we can do it. We really can."

"Together," Tammy said. "And with Robert. Isn't he the greatest?"

Zoe nodded. "He seems very motivational."

To show my solidarity in the world of backyard adventure, I took Zoe's hand. We were like the suckerfish on the belly of a large confused shark. "Super," I said.

"He's very well regarded," Bill said. "In his field."

"I'm sure."

Tammy giggled. She was sweating. It wasn't dainty sweat—nope, she needed a towel. "And we can do it. I know we can." I could see the old Wisconsin cheerleader surfacing.

"We can," Bill agreed.

And then Bill and Tammy hugged us, almost tackled us, as if we had already survived some experience. Their skin smelled of apricots and the beach, their hair a floating trace of smoke, and against all my group-hug instincts, I found my head resting on Bill's shoulder and my arm wrapped around Tammy's waist.

Eventually we separated, and they left us for another couple that wasn't mixing properly. "Walk on coals?" I said to Zoe.

"We're guests."

"I'll put on a silly hat. I'll run wildly with a hopeless kite. But hot coals! That's beyond the call. I don't remember Martha Stewart mentioning any hot-coal-and-canapé party."

And—thank God—Zoe smiled, and for that moment found me amusing again. "You're the worst."

We decided to separate because we hate couples who cling, so she went off in one direction and I went over to Phil Bissel and Chuck Hubert. They were lingering by the coals, both looking defeated.

"No drinks, Mal," Chuck said.

"I heard."

"I can't believe they expect me to walk on fire sober. I mean, with a few drinks, maybe." Chuck reached down and ripped up a clump of grass. "I've done worse." From his palm he picked out single blades and dropped them to the ground. "And no food either."

"What?" I said.

"Nope. We can't eat until we've done the firewalk."

"Bribery," Phil said. He was a fat man who milked his baldness for humor. "There's no way I'm doing it."

"They have champagne when we finish. The good stuff." Chuck grinned. "I might make a sprint for it now." He slipped into a cartoon gesture of running—left leg raised, elbow bent. "Hold me back!"

I stared at the coal bed. It had a mesmerizing effect. I pictured a buried village beneath it—everything laid to waste and eventually covered in ash. "It's a shame to ruin such a nice lawn," I said.

Chuck spat onto the coals. "Oh, you think our man Bill

wouldn't think that through? See those stakes?" He pointed. "That's where the pool is going."

"A pool?"

"Yep, Bill's putting in a pool, has the contractor and everything, and these coals are in the deep end."

"That's smart."

Phil threw an ice cube on the coals. "I don't know what he's thinking," he said. "There's just no chance."

Herb Frankel came over and mimed golf swings. "Boys been playing?"

"No."

He patted me on the back. "How're things? Work all right?"

"Fine." They all knew my job wasn't going well, but some people, like Herb, pretended to empathize, while others just pretended everything was fine.

"It's a tough market. No rhyme or reason. Have to sweat it out." The shimmering coals tinted Herb's face with a red Saran Wrap glow. I imagined him suffocating. "You going to do this shit?"

"I can't imagine."

"How about you, Chuck? A little zombie walk across the coals."

Chuck cringed. He always regretted his drunken performances. "I don't think so." Then he lifted his glass of soft drink. "No booze."

I tried to spot Zoe, but couldn't find her. The sun was down and the night was here and the coals now looked like a very cheap hell that housed very cheap souls. More people came over: the Vollopes and the Burnhams, two couples who always vacationed together; and Leslie Pomeroy, heavily medicated on a new antidepressant. She threw an espadrille onto the coals. It burned quickly, and we all watched.

The man in the asbestos boots stomped over and warned

people not to disturb his spread. "It's essential that it stays pure."

"Are they just briquettes?" someone asked.

"No. We get this stuff from Hawaii."

People were impressed.

I was drinking 7-Up with three wedges of lime, but it didn't fool me. Nothing fooled me. At that moment I knew the ending to every mystery novel, every suspense movie, and all the people around me were stupid. These are moods I get in, most often when I'm driving. No one knows where they're going except me. Standing next to those coals, their bloom quivering against faces, I saw each person as an old man and an old woman, and I saw them alone and waiting and still cold by the fire. I guess it was the gin. I should never drink on an empty stomach.

Zoe appeared at my side. She was holding a Coke. "It's happening soon," she said.

"What?"

"Tammy wants everyone by the coals."

"I wish Ray was sick," I said suddenly.

"Huh?" A look of disgust was on her face.

"Not sick sick, not dying sick. God no. Just sick enough so that we had to stay home."

"Please. Don't get this way."

"Just a little fever, that's all."

"Mal, shut up."

Bill and Tammy Greer walked over with Robert Porterhouse. Bill cleared his throat in a stagy way and everyone hushed. "Well, okay, great. It's great having everyone here, just great. I'm so glad you're all here. Yes. Anyway, it's going to be an exciting night. A bit scary." He chuckled nervously. "But it could be really special. Now I'm going to turn it over to Robert. So here's Robert."

Some people applauded.

Robert Porterhouse loosened his tie. He took off his

jacket and rolled up his sleeves. He smiled a let's-get-down-to-business smile. I was starving. The coals reminded me of the simple cookouts we used to have. Robert gathered us into a tighter circle—it was like camp—and he told us the story of his life.

"My first memory was of fear. The bogeyman. He was an old man with sharp teeth and long dirty fingernails and he was hungry for children. He used to live under my bed. Whenever I wet the sheets, and I did quite often, I would tell my mother that it was the bogeyman. It was impossible for me to go to the bathroom. Why? Because he would've grabbed my ankles and dragged me under. As basic as that. It's that fear that stops us from doing what we really want to do."

I looked around the group. I had to suppress the urge to nudge a few people and make loopy gestures at my head.

"So," he continued, "how do we get over this bogeyman that lives inside of us? Do we turn on the lamp and check under the mattress? Does that solve the problem? No, because we all know that the bogeyman can't be seen in the light. Only in darkness. That's when you see his glowing red eyes and you smell his rotten breath. Sure"—he put his hands in his pockets and paced—"I know what you're saying: those are kids' fears, and as adults we grow out of such fears." He let the last word linger in the air. I felt on the verge of being startled, like when you know that the necking couple in a horror flick is soon to be doomed. "Or do we?" he asked.

The silence lasted even longer this time. Robert knelt down and ran his fingers through the grass. Then he started confessing. "I was twenty-three years old. I flunked out of college. I was a hundred and forty pounds overweight. I had no money. No job. I could barely get up out of bed. In fact, sometimes I spent the whole day in bed. Now what kept me there? What brought me so low? It was fear. I still had that bogeyman under my bed. I still thought that if I took one step I'd be finished."

Fireworks would have been so much more fun. We could have leaned against each other and oohed and aahed at the exploding dandelions and the fluttering snakes.

"How did I break the domination?" He stared at Clare Worden. She was surprised and she smiled and lifted her hands as if she were drying her nail polish. "Well, something bigger than me made me take that step. It was 1989. And there was an earthquake—a pretty big one—and I'm in bed." He began to act out the scene. "Suddenly, my whole apartment collapses, the second floor becomes the first floor. I'm thrown out of bed. I'm in a T-shirt and underwear. And I have to get out. All the windows are broken. There's glass everywhere. A ton of it. I also smell gas. But I still don't move. I'm too scared. And then I hear it, someone crying for help. Then I hear more people crying for help. I know I have to do something. So I concentrate on those cries and I walk and I crawl and I carry those people out of the building. At that moment my mind was completely focused on the task. And I kept on repeating to myself, 'Save Lives. Save Lives.' That day I took five people out of that building. Most of them were elderly, helpless. And when it was all over, and I was wrapped in a blanket and drinking coffee, I didn't have one cut on either foot."

Some peopled sighed in real wonder.

"Is this a miracle?" He shook his head. "Absolutely not. This is the power of the self. At that moment I overcame my fear. I took a step, and with that step the bogeyman disappeared. Now I'm not all that smart. There's nothing 'special' about me. I've just learned a way to align my belief system so that I get what I want. I've empowered myself through positive thinking. Now, I know how this sounds, a whole lot of New Age mumbo jumbo. But I swear to you, and I hope to show you, that with the mind focused, with it directed, there's nothing you can't do. Absolutely nothing."

And for the next hour he tried to convince us that this was all true. He had us doing exercises, meditations, power screams; we played games of trust. I watched Zoe fall into the arms of Jasper Cunningham. Then he fell into her arms. They giggled. Jasper brushed aside his too-long hair and tucked it behind his ears. He acted like a tennis pro. And once again I thought I knew how everything would end. Bill and Tammy orchestrated the activities like amphetamined cruise directors. "Oh, this is fun," they said over and over again. But as time wore on, the rest of us became grumpier and grumpier. "I'm going to pass out," Leslie Pomeroy moaned. The Vollopes and the Burnhams whispered among themselves and hoarded mints. Phil Bissel's baldness radiated defeat and Chuck Hubert was beyond the semblance of life. It was already obvious that no one was going to walk on hot coals, no matter the possible benefits to the soul.

"The heat is over twenty-five hundred degrees Fahrenheit," Robert Porterhouse told us. "Right now it's hotter than the sun."

"Really?" someone said.

"Yes."

People murmured.

"And we will walk on it without burning ourselves. Right?"

"Right."

"Louder."

"Right!" It was one of the first things we had learned: interjections empowered.

Then Robert slipped off his loafers, slipped off his socks. The man with asbestos boots prepared a discreet first aid station which nobody was meant to notice but everyone did. Tammy Greer looked ready to cry into her sweat—she was a liquid special effect—and Bill seemed prepared to drown himself on her shoulder. "Okay," Robert said. "Here I go." A deep breath. Another deep breath. His eyes stared straight ahead, as if they were connected by extension cord to a distant outlet emanating a positive force. "Cool moss, cool moss," he said.

We all chanted along with him. "Cool moss, cool moss."

"Cool moss, cool moss." He goose-stepped across the red-hot coals, his heels kicking up brilliant embers that drifted like the happy fireflies of a summer stroll. But I was waiting for his feet to bubble, for his legs to melt, for this plastic man to scream out, "Oh fuck, was I wrong! Call nine-one-one!" But he kept on moving, and within seconds was finished. He let out a whoop. All of us politely applauded. He rushed over to the group and showed us his feet. They were dirty, a bit pink, but unblistered. "You see, that's the power, that's your power." He was talking excitedly, his exhilaration charging the air. "Your mind can do anything. Absolutely anything!"

People smiled. They nodded. Clare Worden asked if she could touch his foot, and Robert happily obliged. "Unscathed," he said. "Completely unscathed because I didn't let them be scathed. My scathing is my own doing. To be scathed is to be negative. I was scathed. But I will not be scathed again." He practically conjugated that verb for us, and we lingered around the coals like a classroom of uninspired kids listening for the final bell. Empirical evidence was beyond us; we lived in speculation. Some people excused themselves to go to the bathroom. Others were fascinated by their cuticles. Even Bill and Tammy had given up on eagerness and were now in adrenaline detox.

So Robert Porterhouse walked across the coals again. "Cool moss, cool moss," was chanted with the vigor of rote. "Hey, guys," he told us. "That's the power."

The third time he did it people barely noticed. I was standing with Zoe and Jasper. "This is pitiful," Jasper said.

Zoe nodded.

"I mean," he repeated, "just pitiful."

Robert was clapping his hands, patting backs, searching for high-fives. His face was desperate. "C'mon, we can do it," he said.

Herb Frankel heckled, "No, *you* can do it."

People laughed.

Then I slipped off my cheap shoes—I wasn't wearing socks—and started across the coals, a glass of flat 7-Up in my hand. There was silence. No one said, "Cool moss, cool moss." A plane flew overhead, and I wondered if those passengers could see me tread through flame. Maybe they thought that this was an exotic land instead of a prime piece of real estate. Maybe I was a holy man. Maybe I had powers beyond comprehension. Maybe I could transform the elements and turn a hot-coal party into a pool party. So I imagined that I was in the deep end treading toward the shallow end, where a lounge chair floated, a gin and tonic nestled in the drink holder. Mahatma Malachi. Before I began, I was finished.

Robert ran over and hugged me. "Yes. There it is." His face was all relief. "And how are your feet?"

"Fine," I said. I lifted them up. They were covered in ash.

Robert turned to the rest of the group. "See. It can be done."

Chuck Hubert shook my hand. "That's the farthest I've ever seen someone go for a drink."

"Well," Zoe said, "that was interesting."

Robert stayed close to me. I was his first convert. "Don't you feel like you could do anything?"

Now that I was his shill, I said a loud "Yes!"

People still weren't convinced. Robert and I walked across the coals together. Then we did it hand in hand. Soon, we were skipping, but by that time Tammy was locked in her bathroom, Bill was apologizing, and everyone was drinking the champagne and eating the caviar, the toothpick-harpooned shrimp, the sliced ham, the smoked salmon. Robert packed up his motivational devices. "Some people just aren't ready," he told me.

"Yeah," I said.

"But I'm proud of you, Mal."

"Thanks, Dad." I was well into the champagne. "You're not a failure either," I said.

"What?"

"You're not a failure."

"I know that."

When the rum was brought out people cheered, even Robert Porterhouse perked up and after a few mai tais was performing handstands on the lawn. "My center of gravity is perfect," he told Leslie Pomeroy, and she pushed him over and stormed off into the bushes. Hot dogs were roasted. S'mores for dessert. Chuck Hubert somehow got ahold of the asbestos boots and started to do his zombie walk across the coals. There was laughter and applause. Tammy finally came back outside. She was smiling. "Oh, that Chuck," she said. Soon everyone was trying on the boots.

THE PARTY was still in swing when Zoe and I left. Most people had nannies or summer au pairs, while we were lowly with a baby-sitter. The drive home was quicker than the drive there. "How're your feet?" Zoe asked.

"Fine."

"I still can't believe you did that. Crazy."

I concentrated on the corridor of light and tried to keep the car within it.

"You of all people," she said.

"Did you have a good time?" I said.

"It was ridiculous."

"Yeah." I didn't even try to make her laugh.

When we got home the TV was on and Gwen was lying on the couch watching a late-night movie. She quickly got up. I wanted to help her with that head. "Hi," she said.

"Hey," Zoe said. She leaned against a chair. "Everything go all right?"

"No problem. A little tears in *Chitty Chitty Bang Bang*, but otherwise, fine."

I said, "The child catcher, right?"

"Yeah."

I walked over to the bar and made myself a proper drink. "Poor Ray hates that creepy guy. 'Children,' " I called out in a shrill voice. " 'Candies and sweets and lollipops.' "

Gwen giggled.

"But he was good?" I asked.

"Just fine."

"Good."

Zoe sighed and then abruptly said, "Well, I guess Mr. Scott will drive you home." She made her way upstairs. "Sorry we're so late."

"No problem."

GWEN didn't live very far away.

"Did you have a good time?" she asked me.

"It was all right. Same old stuff."

The sporadic oncoming traffic lit the inside of the car, transforming Gwen's face into a second moon. And still wired from the party, I wanted to talk, wanted to tell her something wise, something profound, something that would help her better understand this awkward life. "You know my grandmother and grandfather used to live out on this island in Maine," I said. "A beautiful spot. Coastal. Islands all around. Really beautiful. And on one of the islands these adolescent kids would get dropped off for three days of survival. On their own, you know."

"Take a left," Gwen said.

"Here?"

"Yeah."

The headlights, like prison searchlights, ran by a corner house.

"Anyway, it was some sort of Outward Bound program. Leadership skills and all that crap." I glanced at her quickly. "You know, where you're given something like a hook and fishing line and five matches and a knife. That's it. With that you have to make do."

"A right." She was carefully watching the street.

"Right?"

"Uh-huh."

"Well, I used to visit my grandparents during the summer. It was great. Really nice."

"Sounds it," Gwen said.

"And my grandparents had this sailboat, and we sailed around quite a bit. Always sailing."

"Okay." Gwen sagged forward. I thought something might be wrong. A stomach cramp. A contraction. Her hands rested on the dashboard. "You're going to want to take a right pretty soon. The next right. It pops out of nowhere."

"Got it," I said. "A right. Anyway, I remember the three of us making sandwiches in the morning, a ton of them, and we'd seal them in little plastic bags and pack them with us when we went sailing. And off we'd go. And we'd sail to this survival island, and my grandfather would sound the foghorn."

She said, "This right."

"Here?"

"Yeah."

I made the turn. I wondered if the people inside the corner house could see the headlights dash across the walls, if they woke up frightened at the possibility of escaped convicts, or if maybe they dreamed about being in jail for an unknown crime they didn't commit. "Well, it was unreal," I said.

"What's that?"

"The survival island. It was unreal. These kids would come out from the woods, just emerge from the woods all cut up and covered in bites. They looked miserable, almost beaten, you know, like they were in over their heads. But seeing us they'd smile and wave and wade into the water, and we'd toss out the sandwiches—ham and cheese, turkey, roast beef, chicken salad, egg salad, tomato and cheese—and soon these kids were having a picnic on the rocks."

"Okay, after this street take the next street left." Gwen pointed to the distant spot.

"Left?"

"Yep. On Musgrove."

"Musgrove. Left on Musgrove." I leaned my elbow out the window. In front of houses, sprinklers clicked across lawns—my favorite sound—and some of them swept the edge of the road like a scythe stretched to its limit. The car seemed suddenly loud, as if low beams and high beams screamed through the night, so I reached down and just turned the headlights off. There. Darkness was no longer cheated. The sky was everywhere, the stars visible, the space between objects flattened.

Gwen didn't say a word; she didn't move.

"A left?" I asked.

"Yeah."

I stared out at the suburban silhouettes: a few porch lights glowing, a few blue shimmerings from bedroom and living-room televisions. Landmarks—a comforting word—landmarks to shore yourself against a mysterious world. And for a moment, things felt present. My friends were my friends and my wife was my wife and my feet did not burn.

I flipped down the indicator. It clicked along with the sprinklers outside.

Remote Feed

I

*When not frightened, they slowly crawl along with
their tails and bellies dragging on the ground. They
often stop, and doze for a minute or two, with closed
eyes, and hind legs spread out on the parched soil.*

—CHARLES DARWIN

The three of them have been quiet for the last hour.
Tired. Their bodies tired. Their conversation tired. That
happens with the seventh drink. Something about the seventh drink. It's like the onslaught of middle age, depressing,
disheartening, you can't believe you've arrived at this particular spot. But you slog through. An eighth drink. A ninth
drink. And—boom!—at the ten-drink mark you change and
you accept this life you've made for yourself, a perfectly fine
life, a solid life, and in the end a life you can't do anything
about. But these guys, at present, are stuck in the midlife crisis of the seventh drink.

Zev has almost completely given up, his right cheek
planted on crossed elbows. Uneven snores bubble from his
drooling mouth, similar to a Saint Bernard in the midst of a
nightmare. But he's always doing that, slumping wherever
he can, on park benches, against walls. A passerby might
think he has just heard awful news.

McGraw is next to him, busy trying not to see his own reflection in the bottle-lined mirror behind the bar. To be a vampire would be cool, he imagines, an invisible presence, with only your consequences being felt. He reaches for a pack of cigarettes, his finger extending the same way God, or Adam—he can't remember which—extends his finger on the Sistine ceiling.

Nearby, Lewis leans forward and smiles his smile at the bartender. It is a well-designed smile, cultivated over the years into an openmouthed smile, not too toothy, not crooked. All in all it's a smile of good faith that says, Nothing up my gums, no secrets in my cheeks. And the tongue is always ready with a kind word while the hand reaches for the wallet. "Bueno country here, muy bueno, mi amigo," he says, as if he really speaks the language. By now he has his wallet out, that thick piece of leather so impressive to the Third World, and he's handing over a laminated ID to the bartender. This is the part of the job that Lewis loves, saying the following words the same way James Bond says his name. "Press." He pauses. "CNN News."

"Press?"

"Sí. We're here to do a little story." After decades in the business, Lewis never specifies the details of anything. That way everyone is on guard, everyone is helpful, and everyone bends over backward because everyone, from a coat-check girl to the President of the United States, thinks the story is about the twisted world they inhabit. It can also sometimes get him a free drink.

"For the First Lady's arrival?" the bartender asks.

Lewis reluctantly confirms the hunch. "Sí, mi amigo." No need to be secretive, this isn't a scoop. The First Lady of the United States is coming here. A short stay. A little reprieve from Washington. She's always wanted to visit the Galápagos Islands—her statement to the press—a place of origins, a place of beauty, a place of scientific discovery, a place like no other place in the world. Unique. So Lewis and crew have been sent over to cover her brief journey. For them, it's a working vacation. A deserved break. Just soft news wrapped up in a twenty-second kicker at the end of a newscast. There's no reason for a reporter to be dragged along. Besides, their man Laraby is dead anyway.

Lewis checks on the state of his colleagues and figures that "we need another drink, a muy macho one."

The bartender smiles. "How about a Guy Fawkes?"

"Qué's that?"

"A bomb that'll blow you away."

"Sounds bueno. Tres, por favor."

No hurry in his movement, the bartender sets out three glasses, each one shaped like a gunpowder keg. He packs in crushed ice and then pours in the contents of various bottles: rum, vodka, triple sec, tequila, orange and cranberry juice. When all mixed up and ready to go, the straw stands as straight as a fuse.

"The Emergency Broadcasting System," Lewis calls out to the other two, his voice a monotone bugle. *"This is not a test, I repeat, this is not a test. The end is near. The bombs are falling.* You know, just once I'd like to hear that."

McGraw slaps Zev a few times—it's the only way to wake him. Zev stirs with the speed of an ugly flower blooming. Seeing the drink in front of him—what a funny glass!—he picks it up and deep-throats half of the brown liquid. "Ka-boom," he whispers. It doesn't take much to envision this huge man as a mythical Titan with a hogshead of mead. Or a Hollywood bodyguard with that blond ponytail and a face as big as a spare tire. He toasts, "Pozovite kola za hitnu pomoc," to the three of them, having forgotten any sense of procedure.

"What the hell's that mean?"

"Call a fucking ambulance," is the Serbo-Croatian translation. Zev loves to inhabit his English with a herd of free-roaming expletives.

A fresh load of tourists enters the airport bar. Many are American, but many are German and many are Australian and quite a few are Dutch. They take the tables, dumping cameras and sunblock on the highly polished surfaces, removing Panama hats, sunbonnets, pith helmets, baseball caps that have molded a slight tonsure into their bleached-blond, permed, mop-topped, feather-cut hair. Everyone here is ready to be Saint Francis. Or Doctor Doolittle. They all let out deep sighs, almost in unison, as if a forced march has been completed, the ball and chain of carry-on luggage resting at their feet.

McGraw lights up another cigarette, one of the supreme joys in his life. The tobacco cloud seems, for a second, to sublimate his flesh from a painfully obvious solid—stubby limbs, bad skin, dandruff—into a mysterious vapor. He inhales and pauses, licking his lips, and then blows out a casual blast, imagining within the whirlwind whole trailer parks sucked up and spinning. He stares at the lava red of the cigarette; the barely burning paper is lovely. The smoke unfurls from the glowing ash the same way gossamer shoots from a spider's anus. That's an attribute Spider-Man was lucky to avoid. Everyone would be disgusted, no matter how many times you saved Manhattan from the evil Dr. Octopus. The theme song to the afternoon cartoon— "Spider-Man, Spider-Man, does whatever a spider can"— begins to loop in his head.

Growing up, McGraw lived for comic books, his room cluttered with stacks of colored newsprint. But he wasn't crazy about the superheroes or supervillains. They were boring, all identical except for their particular gimmicks. No, he loved the secret identities, the people they pretended to be—Bruce Wayne, Peter Parker, Dr. Bruce Banner—normal joes with that hidden power to influence a planet. Anytime. Anywhere. And even though somewhere in the world a tragedy happened every second of every day, sometimes Clark Kent let it slide and didn't listen with super-hearing and didn't look with super-vision. Nope. Instead, he went to work, earned a measly living as a reporter, and turned in puff pieces while children screamed in fast flaming fires.

"Some chasers," Lewis is suggesting. "The second wave of the attack is on. Commander Zev, you order the counter-strike."

"Sta?"

"Get us some beer."

"Ja bih tri pivo, molim."

"Speak Spanish, you asshole. Do your job for a change."

After fumbling through his Berlitz phrase book, Zev spits out, "Tomaré tres cervezas, por favor." The pronunciation is awful, like a ventriloquist trying to do a bit with water in his mouth.

"Man, you're hopeless," Lewis tells him.

"Fuck your teeth."

McGraw changes his order to a Bloody Mary, and sitting there, he begins to think to himself in a bad Transylvanian accent, rolling over the r's, slamming shut the k's. He has it all figured out. A superhero vampire—by day he processes film in a newspaper's darkroom; it's always night in there and has the chemical smell of a casket leaking embalming fluid. And when the sun goes down, he rights the wrongs on the front-page photos. The murdered heiress. The oil spill. The gangster acquitted on a technicality. Murrow—that'd be his name—would shuck his lab clothes for a black outfit, tastefully done, with a trench coat as cape. And the next morning, he'd feign ignorance at the newly developed pic-tures, at the newly bannered headlines, at the do-good deeds of the night angel they call Murrow. Then again, maybe it's too much like Batman. And what if all of those villains became part of the undead? That wouldn't be too useful.

A captain and co-captain enter the bar. Neither wears a uniform, except both have those large mustaches favored by terrorists and pilots alike. Stewardesses follow closely behind. Their conversation sounds flirty, but in Spanish everything sounds flirty.

Zev asks the bartender about the Spanish word for cunt, pussy, twat, you know, pastrmku, you know, polu-peceno sunku, you know, vagina.

"Coño," the bartender mutters.

"Coño." Zev consults his phrase book. "¿Dónde está el coño más cercano, por favor?" He thumbs through a page. "¿Se puede ir andando?"

The bartender smiles. They all have a good laugh—Lewis just pretending to understand—while a voice comes over the loudspeaker and speaks in five different languages.

II

They inhabit burrows . . . One front leg for a short time scratches up the soil, and throws it towards the hind foot, which is well placed so as to heave it beyond the mouth of the hole. That side of the body being tired, the other takes up the task, and so on alternately.

—CHARLES DARWIN

But before this, before the Galápagos, about two weeks before, there is Sarajevo and there is the death of Richard Laraby, the reporter, the tall blond stud who used to play quarterback for Georgia Tech. He doesn't die live. No, it's taped. But they tape everything. Then they edit. Then they transmit the finished story back to Atlanta. That's their day, a two-minute-and-thirty-second report. A little blood, a little suffering, a little gunplay, then bring on the drinks and maybe tonight a little hash. But sometimes Laraby will do a live follow-up, a real pain, and at three in the morning he'll stand in the alley behind the Hilton, freezing his nuts off, and he'll answer softball questions about the spirit of the Sarajevo people. "There is a haunted look on their faces," he'll say in the headlights of the camera, the Southern tic trained out of his voice. "Their eyes well past desperation and much closer to death itself. And like the city behind me, dark now, its scars hidden, only a semblance of humanity remains." This, in fact, is an apt description of Laraby and Lewis and McGraw, the three of them huddling in that alley, the only safe place to kick up the generator and the mercury lights. Tonight, the network wants the word "Live" tagged to the vanity corner of the screen. The falling snow will be an added bonus. A nice touch. And it will film beautifully, the flakes creating an optical effect of movement so that if you relax your eyes a bit, Laraby seems to lift slowly into the air. It wouldn't take much. The man is losing weight, everybody can see that, and his clothes are starting to look absurdly ill-fitted.

"They're getting letters," Lewis tells him at dinner. They're sitting in the main restaurant at the Hilton, every table filled with members of the world press. The Hilton, except for the gaping hole on the top two floors, has been doing great business. A new Babel. Much better than the Winter Olympics.

"Letters?"

"About your weight. I guess people are worried. They want you to eat."

Laraby lifts up a forkful of rice and beans. A pile of stringy meat, zebra flanks that Zev managed to hustle up from the condemned zoo, remains untouched along the edge. "Well," he says, "next time bring on the monkey. Yum yum."

Lewis reaches into his leather sidebag and pulls out a handful of mini chocolate bars, treats he gives to kids who pose in rubble. "Just put on some weight."

With surprising quickness, McGraw snatches one of the

candies, but the movement still feels wasted. Telekinesis would be so much purer, the mind's tentacles grabbing on to the things you need while the useless body shrivels below the neck. McGraw has lost weight as well, about ten pounds in the last year. God knows where it comes from, the guy's already a rail. Still, he enjoys the lessening, even though this winter his skin is starting to turn a shade of light blue—not a good sign—and the camera's feeling a bit heavy. "What time do we go?" he asks, the chocolate doing somersaults in his mouth.

"Three-thirteen A.M. We have the fourth spot."

Laraby nods. This is a great opportunity, this ongoing story, this constant coverage for the last year, and the public's growing familiarity with his face. At least four times a week he files a report. There's Laraby standing next to the destroyed cathedral, mosque, temple. There's Laraby in front of the Olympic oval now used as a mass graveyard. "The Siege of Sarajevo"—the network's bloody banner—belongs solely to Laraby, and he's a hit. Number one with a bullet. Back home, mainly in the South, a fan club has started up; they call themselves Larababes and they flood CNN with letters asking about this new reporter: Is he married? No, recently divorced. How old is he? Thirty-two years old. How tall? Six feet one. What denomination? Baptist. But about a month ago, the letters began to change: He looks pale! Feed him! He needs some color! Bring him home, poor thing!

"I think you also need a haircut," Lewis adds.

Laraby runs his hands through his greasy hair. This is certainly the longest it's ever been, a good two inches below the ear, but he's enjoying the look. "I don't know."

"On camera you're getting a bit mangy."

"You think?"

"Yeah."

"Okay."

"Good."

Lewis usually gets his way. He's the veteran producer, a legend in the field and a witness to over twenty years of conflict. Algeria to Zaire, a passport as thick as a phone book, that's what he'll tell you if you're next to him at a party. What he won't tell you is that he'd probably be a reporter if he weren't so funny-looking. Long neck. No chin. A pinhead a few degrees fatter than a sideshow freak. All he has is that smile, that great smile, and a voice that can talk anyone into anything. Just ask his three ex-wives.

Outside it's quiet, the shelling on temporary hiatus, but people still huddle over their food in case dust starts to fall. Most of the tables are in the process of a long drink, no live shot for them tonight, the story bagged and tagged, and Zev goes over to the French correspondents to get a hit of hash. Everyone smokes Turkish hash, sent over by the Muslim brethren. "Fucking puis-je voir la carte?" says Zev, slapping a few loose hands.

McGraw watches Zev take a long puckered drag from a pipe, watches Zev look over at him and smile, the smoke slowly curling out of his turnip-sized nostrils. To the bat cave, McGraw says to himself, and he gives Zev the finger and lights up a cigarette. "Are we in the alley?" he asks Lewis.

"Yeah. Though I'd love to get on the roof somehow, especially if there's some good shelling." Lewis nods. "That'd be a great shot—Laraby on the fucking roof as the city explodes behind him."

Laraby, of course, agrees. He agrees to everything Lewis suggests. At first it was a problem. A bit apprehensive, he wanted to keep his distance. Back in the States Laraby covered natural disasters, that was his gig, his first stint being hurricane Hugo in '89. He impressed people with his compassion, and as he toured Charleston, chunks of roof in his path, trees snapped over in tragic supplication, he spoke to the camera and said, "What Sherman once spared, Hugo has damned." Fucking poetry. And the woman showing him around, a blond coed at The College of Charleston, her name an old Southern name that rhymes with lots-of-dough, she fell in love with him a few minutes before he fell in love with her. Weeks later the San Francisco earthquake hit. Then the California fires. Hurricane Andrew. When the dust cleared from those crazy three years, Laraby, the new golden boy, had been married, cheated on, lied to, and divorced—Jesus, you can be fooled!—and he was now ready to visit the site of a public Armageddon.

"We need something big," Lewis is saying. "People are getting bored with the same old stuff."

"Yeah?"

"It's got to get sexier."

This is true. Same old stuff, that's a huge danger. Fresh angles are important, fresh ways of telling this story. Maybe a profile on the upcoming production of *Hair*. Or how about something ironic on the Museum of the Revolution. You can't just have mortar shells and rubble and blood, mothers' breaking down over the day's corpses. There has to be context, no matter how powerful the image. Hell, McGraw has stacks of unusable videos, each shot more horrific than the next. Postmortems floating down the Sava River. Hanged men and boys festooning trees. Women beating themselves to kill the product of rape. You can't believe what you see—it seems so unreal—and in the end you don't want to believe it. No way. Instead, you turn it into fiction with well-done special effects. And the actors are so good, it's scary. This abstraction gives you distance and control, and sleep acts as a commercial break. "Now back to our regularly scheduled war, already in progress," is one of Lewis's favorite lines. But this isn't working for Laraby. Things are slipping into an absurd equation where he's equivalent with Sarajevo. Each atrocity is part of his own evolution, almost like childhood memories recovered by a spurious quack, and he watches and rewatches the unwatchable videos, sometimes staying up all night in front of the monitor—Did this really happen? Of course it did— over and over again. There's the zoo, a lovely old thing, built a hundred years ago, and today its animals are getting butchered for much-needed meat. The monkey house is a den of almost-human screams. Dead elephants are chain-sawed for their flesh. The untender birds, mostly carrion, are freed to starve on their own or to scavenge off those unclaimed. Jesus. These images flicker through the sleepless night like a nightmare. It isn't cruelty—you have to tell yourself that—it's awful necessity. The keeper, a haggard man twenty-five years with this zoo, aims the shotgun at the caged tiger's head. Nothing to be done. Laraby hits rewind, play, rewind again. A loop to the polar bears. The footage is purposeless. No one wants to see it. Too much grit for back home. Plus the fearful lack of civility, the giant leap of regression, all that crap is a bummer to a humanist nation. But Zev, through his many connections, has managed to scramble up some zebra meat for the four of them. It's tough, charbroiled to a pale brown, but they eat most of it. Except for Laraby.

"You know, I once drank bat's blood in Cambodia," Lewis says, beginning to spill his usual stories of Disgusting Meals Eaten. "That was the worst."

McGraw disagrees. "But they're bats," he says. "Who gives a shit about a bat?"

"It tasted awful."

The three of them are sipping peppermint schnapps, a rarity here. Zev found it on the black market, a whole case. He also found a jar of Hellmann's mayonnaise and ten rolls of Italian toilet paper, Di Prima Classe, a soft two-ply brand. A sufficiently stoned Zev walks back to the table, his eyes pink, his grouper mouth sucking in air. He tops off their glasses, greeting them with, "Ziveli. And how is the zebra tonight?"

"Excellent."

"Dobro, vrlo dobro." He's been their translator for a couple of months—the old translator, a guy named Alija, suffered a nervous breakdown from his sister's death—and Zev wants to keep this job for as long as possible. It pays well. There are benefits. And the Hilton has no more need for an assistant concierge.

"Anyway," Lewis continues, "they bring the bat to your table, holding it by the wings so you can see the wingspan. That's very important for some reason. Then they whack it a good one on the head and bleed it into a glass. It's meant to be a delicacy."

"Why drink it?"

"Keeps your dick hard for a week."

"Cat's the worst thing I ever ate," McGraw says. "The family cat. Snowball."

"Sta?"

"My father kind of flipped out and did some terrible things." McGraw immediately regrets bringing up this memory, of his father serving dinner, those greasy pieces of kitty meat, to his wife and kids, and forcing the six of them to clean their plates.

"The family cat?" Lewis shakes his head, like a bowling pin uncertain of falling. "That's cold. I've eaten cat and dog—in fact, I've probably eaten just about every variety of pet there is—but never the family pet, or a family pet. That's . . . that's bad. Anyone ever see that movie *King Rat?*"

No one has. Laraby is still thinking about bat's blood and a day-long boner. Would that be pleasurable? And then his mind settles on cruel tortures he used to inflict on the neighborhood animals: throwing rocks at dogs; putting two cats in a potato sack; blowing up seagulls with M-8os. Why do you do those things?

"Was your cock?" Zev asks.

"What?"

"Your fucking cock." Zev gestures to his groin and makes an adaptation of a fascist salute.

"Nada." Lewis refills his glass, hoping nobody sees him drink this candy booze. Disgusting. And the translator pours with such a maître d' flourish and clinks glasses every chance he gets. "The family cat. How the hell was it cooked?"

McGraw pretends not to hear. He stares into the zebra meat—Sheena, Queen of the Jungle, had a zebra for wheels, kind of a pet, though McGraw isn't too fond of the whole noble-savage motif in comics. Except Conan. And he says, "Why didn't they let the tiger loose in the Serengeti pen? That would've been something."

"A Bengal," Zev answers. "Fucking Indian, not African."

"Let him stretch his legs one last time. Let him get a taste of the old country. Let him hunt and chase and rip apart. That would've been something to see. Instead of the shotgun." McGraw slides the meat into his mouth: the kill.

The animal would probably just sit there, stuck with a new fear, too scared of those high-to-the-ground creatures. No doubt. Fifteen years in the zoo, sleeping and eating, cooled off in the summer and kept warm in the winter, you forget the real you and fall into a different you, a you without need, a you without painful realizations. But who says this isn't the life to lead? The four of them basically agree.

"But it'd be nice to show your real power."

The tiger didn't move as the keeper took aim. Did he know? A stupid question. It's not like being pursued, adrenaline pumping, running because genetically you have to run until those claws swipe your hind quarters and you fall and tumble and within seconds you hear things tear and you feel things spill and you know things are over. No, the tiger didn't flinch. McGraw held the close-up on the face, a brutal shot, and off-camera you could hear the click of the pump action and the crazy moaning of the keeper. Boom. That was one heavy-duty gun. And Laraby had the perfect copy: executions, like zoos, are the sole property of humans. Then the tiger shook as if shocked and backed itself in the corner, blood all over the place. Every great city has a zoo.

"And you ate the cat." Lewis is still fixated. He can get that way, waltz with a thought through a whole set of topics.

"Yeah."

"Was it off the bone at least?"

"I really can't remember."

Outside the shelling starts again, the hills raining mortars on the entrenched city. This noise makes Laraby nervous, he can't quite get used to it, and though there's no danger of a possible hit—the Serbs are targeting the southern section—he stops eating and looks up at the ceiling. Things quiver slightly. The silverware on the plates. The hanging lights. Like the nearing of a merciless army from Megiddo. Frightening. With natural disasters he had arrived after the fact, the destruction laid out in front of him. Except the fires. The fires he had witnessed, but it was always from a distance and it was always beautiful. The fires he had actually enjoyed. Certain colors only exist in fire—he discovered this early on, as a kid, a little pyro with his father's stolen lighter. Let's burn this. And sometimes he'd cut his fingernails and cut clumps of his hair, and he'd burn that in a small pile. An awful stench of himself emerged, sweet and thick and oily.

"But wait," Lewis asks. "Did you know it was Snowball?"

"Not really. I don't know. Let's drop it, okay?"

The shells hit in clockwork fashion. And Laraby listens intently. It isn't that he imagines screams—that sensation will come later—but it's something else, a different noise, as when you hear voices, in the shower, in an airplane's engine, in an electric shaver, and the voices are calling for you, trying to find you. An eerie feeling. And as Laraby spends more time in this city, a weird place of diffuse civilizations and bloods held in the sexless crotch of the hills, the voices become louder.

"Did you puke when you found out?"

"No, okay."

Zev pulls out hash from his inside pocket. "Do you guys want to smoke?"

McGraw—"Yes"—quickly answers.

The seals were particularly hard to kill. The tank drained of the long-neglected water, green for months, but the seals were quick and they hid in the large rock formation that acted as their artificial home. The keeper slipped on the slimy bottom, his shotgun discharging in the air. A crowd of reporters gathered. The animals barked and pushed themselves deeper into the crevices. They knew what was coming—dying screams don't need to be translated from species to species. Laraby leaned over the rail, his feet bobbing up and down. The whole scene was almost comical. A few of them were easy to kill; they were older and lazier and almost let the gun rest against their sleek heads. But the rest were a bitch: seals from an overcrowded Scottish zoo, North Sea seals. The keeper had trouble with their upland names—Macgregor, Glasgow—and it all sounded absurd, not just his pronunciation, but his trying to coax them out while blood pooled at his feet. But he had a fish, a rubber fish, one of those novelty gifts. He waved it in the air, as if teasing for a trick. The reward. Laraby glanced about in shock. Lewis and McGraw were, as usual, side by side, like a drummer and a bass player in a wedding band. Zev was off with one of the other keepers—they were shooting the pigeons that lingered by the fountains. Just the other day parents and children were coming to this zoo to try to forget themselves. Now the seals were the only ones left—four of them, to be exact—each wedged in the hollow of the middle, each hungry for even a fake herring.

A thick smoke joins the air. For a second Laraby thinks
he's smelling himself burn, or maybe others. McGraw passes
the pipe to Lewis. "The cat"—he shakes his head—"just
blows me away."

"Shut up."

"This the fucking best," says Zev. "Trust me. You can
function, no fucking problem. Look, I juggle." He picks up
three rolls of Di Prima Classe.

The remaining seals were eventually killed and skinned,
their blubber used for burning oil, their fatty meat fed to
children. The butcher did everything by guesswork, though
he was completely baffled by the giraffes. And McGraw
captured all of it on tape.

They taped everything. Even Laraby's death. Still long-
haired and thin, and quiet for the last couple of days before
he died. Something was bothering him, that's what the three
of them would say later. He was depressed. Or just lonely. Distant. Who knows? But as he interviewed a woman about her
prized collection of porcelain plates—"It's a miracle that
none of your things have broken during the incessant
shelling"—Laraby rubbed his head, his temple, his left eye,
and within seconds his appendages, including ears, felt as
if they were retracting into his skull in a blinding flash. His last
thought: Spontaneous combustion! Right here! What a way
to go! And then he collapsed on the living-room floor. A
plate was taken down with him—a commemorative Royal
Wedding plate, 1956, the Prince and Princess of Monaco
posed in the center—but he cradled it safely to his chest, like
a lover's picture, Grace peeking over his arm. Cause of
death: an aneurysm. Expired in less than a minute. The
woman, wearing her best clothes and a ton of makeup,
crouched over him and tried to prod him back to life while
McGraw kept shooting and Zev considered taking a hockey
stick to this fragile place and Lewis wished, for an instant,
that it could have been a sniper's bullet that brought down his

reporter, or a devastating mortar, or an angry mob pissed off at America's indifference. Something sexy with legs.

III

I watched one for a long time, till half its body was buried; I then walked up and pulled it by the tail; at this it was greatly astonished, and soon shuffled up to see what was the matter; and then stared me in the face, as much as to say, "What made you pull my tail?" . . . I threw [it] . . . as far as I could, into a deep pool left by the retiring tide.

— CHARLES DARWIN

This isn't a paradise. More like a barbecue on the verge of igniting. The airport's tarmac smells of spilled diesel, and the distant lava, long hardened, menaces with spent fury à la late Joan Crawford. The First Lady's a bit late. Nothing new. It's around five in the afternoon. Still hot. Not much of a breeze. The sun is giving no hints of ever leaving the sky, and the earth, or this fat part bulging at the seam, sucks it up with forced devotion. It could be autumn, winter, spring, or summer. The weather never changes.

A crowd has gathered, about sixty people corralled behind a wooden barricade. The front line belongs to the press, print and TV, mostly South American, ready to capture the taxiing of the airplane and the eventual disembarking of the First Lady. Behind them are second-tier dignitaries too lowly to greet anyone. Plus a few naturalists and soldiers thrown into the mix. Finally, toward the back, children and young women act as filler, their small American flags lazy at their sides. A floral mélange of tourists has also joined them, but these individuals look out of place, as if they were hostages waylaid en route to a Club Med.

Everyone is staring into flat blue space.

The camera their locus, Lewis, McGraw and Zev stand

unsteadily together, press credentials fastened to their pants. Against protocol, their shirts are off because it's hot and they're not used to being hot and having their shirts off. It makes them happy even though a lot of the tourists bitch about the constant heat. But what do you expect? It's the fucking equator. The guys laugh at this. They've been laughing for the last hour—setting up the tripod, talking to the advance crew, meeting the reporter from *Brasilia Today*—laughing because everything seems so funny. Except the flying cockroaches.

"Jesus, I hate these things!" Lewis shrieks. One of the bugs has landed on his head, the creature's podites getting caught in his curly hair. With spastic motions he quickly sweeps it off. "Where'd it go?"

"Fucking what?" Zev asks.

"The cockroach."

"I hate those things," says McGraw.

"Dammit, that's not fair." Lewis tenses his jaw and turbans his shirt around his head. "Bastard's uncatchable." But that's what happens when you have no natural predators—you develop hobbies, like flying. Lewis hates such insectile advancement. Plain cockroaches are bad enough, but when they're airborne it seems positively postapocalyptic. And who started doomsday and didn't tell him? What's next? Dog-walking fleas . . . dieting tapeworms . . . hair-styling lice. As a kid he sometimes had problems getting to sleep, imagining the millions of microbes nibbling on his body, the amoebas dining in his intestines, his flesh nothing more than a take-out meal. "Why the hell do they have to fly?" Lewis asks.

McGraw answers with a "Why not?"

"Rats don't fly."

"Fucking pigeons," Zev says.

"More like bats. I think bats are closer to rats and so they'd be considered the flying rat."

"It rhymes at least."

"No," Zev interrupts. "Bats are fucking mammals. Closer to us. Pigeons are flying rats. No bullshit, trust me. I killed enough to know. They're stupid and dirty, circling those fountains until they're all fucking dead and on the ground. And the women still happy for food." This ends the conversation. Zev's gravy-thick voice has a way of doing this. Everything he says sounds so tragic and final.

An airplane breaks through the blue and someone shouts and points to the sky like a sailor on the prow of the *Pinta*. Soon everyone is shouting and pointing to the sky. The airplane begins to descend, its wheels locked down and ready to grasp the ground. The people are so excited, you'd think it's the first time they've seen such a thing.

Lewis wonders how Laraby would've described it—the glittering metal, the anticipation. Back home, his death was received with little fanfare. The autopsy betrayed a congenital condition, a hidden glitch he was born with, and it was just a matter of time before the bug in the brain burst to life. Sure, there was coverage, his photograph and his dates, a brief homage to his brief career, the anchor concluding the report with *our-prayers-are-with-his-family*. But that was it. They didn't even show the video of his brief spasms, his rolled-back eyes, his grimaced mouth. Too morbid, they told Lewis. No need to turn it into a tabloid event. But if it had been a bullet that ripped through his brain instead of an arterial dilatation, if the blood had been all external instead of internal, shooting into the air like the blood of that poor bastard in Vietnam, the gun-to-the-head guy, then maybe it would've been the lead story, a special report, a bulletin. No parachute journalism—jump in, tape the segment, and take the next flight home—but a literal deadline, a perfect mix of subjective and objective news, a reporter as victim, as casualty, as sacrifice to the event itself. In the end, Lewis felt gypped, like a boy robbed of the game-winning hit because the pitcher threw a tricky strike.

The plane lands with the finesse of an albatross—*bump, bump, thud*—then turns and taxis toward the specified greeting zone.

"What are you going to do?" Lewis asks McGraw.

"It's pretty difficult."

"Get her deplaning. That's our establishing shot."

"Of course."

Lewis consults a clipboard even though it tells him nothing. The logistics are not complex. Just follow her around. Watch her linger next to the sea lions, her face all smiles at their aquatic adorableness. Watch her mourn the short cruel life of baby turtles, only one ever makes it. Watch her laugh at the marine iguanas, so prehistoric, so bizarre, as they swim with their tails sweeping the water, their heads poking from the surface the same way Mother laps the community pool. Watch her take note of the saddle-back tortoise, steadfast and consistent, like a politician she knows.

"Molim, a little rest," says Zev before slumping to the ground, his huge body falling the way Robert Mitchum used to fall, with reluctant inevitability. "Fucking sleep," he mutters. Arms curl around the hot metal of the tripod, hands lock, and he looks up and imagines, for a frozen second, that he's being trampled by a lethargic crowd. At least there are no pigeons here.

The plane, a customized 727, eases to a stop. Engines rev down in a fading tone, almost mournful. After the gangway is affixed to the fuselage's front door, the red carpet is rolled out. That's when the taped music begins to play, something by Sousa, and the little flags—plastic Stars and Stripes stapled to dowels—are lifted and flapped, each one designed to sustain maximum enthusiasm at cheapest cost.

Lewis thinks about moving the camera back a bit and placing some children in the lower foreground, blurry yet eager, the tops of their heads bouncing with glee. But what's the point? Right now he doesn't feel like moving. Not ever.

Not in a million years. Not until something has changed in him. A new adaptation. An Elegant head. A solid chin. Trustworthy eyes.

The door opens.

Starting to film, McGraw centers on the door. If in some backward countries a photograph steals your soul, what the hell would this do? He could wreak havoc with the tribes of the rain forest, all without destroying a single thing. Video-man.

After a while, two secret service agents emerge, their habits ingrained in everyone's head: dark glasses, plain suits, fingers in ear, mouths to sleeve; they take the stairs with suspicion. Then the First Lady emerges, waving hand first, followed by a genuine smile of It's-great-to-be-here-in-the-Galápagos. She pauses at the top, her khaki outfit perfect for these parts.

"Holy shit." A jolt moves through Lewis. "Are you getting this?"

"Yeah."

"It's a miracle." Moving closer to the camera, wanting to be sure it's working, trying not to step on Zev. "I can't believe this. It's better than the *Challenger*."

The First Lady descends.

"Get the legs."

"Sure."

"But don't make it obvious."

She's wearing shorts, maybe for the first time since becoming First Lady. Not maybe, definitely. Because look at those legs! Blotchy white skin, some of it curdled, pouring out of khaki. Thighs as big as pillows. Bowed knees that probably haven't touched since she was a teenager. Shins? There are no shins, only calves.

"I had no idea," Lewis says. He feels something on his shoes. It's Zev resting his head. "I knew about the ankles. But not this."

The First Lady greets the people waiting below, shaking hands with dignitaries and accepting flowers from a nervous girl, a tiny thing, who starts to cry uncontrollably, her face creased with five-year-old misery.

"The networks are going to shoot themselves for missing this. So are the tabloids. I bet they open with this, or maybe not this, but they'll get to this sooner rather than later. *Inside Edition, Hard Copy,* they'd start right here. Get some fitness experts, maybe the Buns of Steel woman. Or Richard Simmons could do his shtick, driving up to the White House in the Deal-a-Meal van."

The First Lady picks up the girl, the girl's arm wrapping around her neck, the girl's face burying under her chin. They rock together.

"Really go tight on the gams."

"How tight?"

"To the flesh. I want to see everything."

McGraw zooms in with terrifying speed, pushing aside any distance with a mere touch of his finger.

"I want to see the pulse in the varicose veins," whispers Lewis, his body beginning to sway. "The horror of cellulite. Tighter. Tighter. Tighter."

The crowd cheers.

Anaconda Wrap

> *Do you not know that the unrighteous will not inherit the kingdom of God? Do not be deceived; neither the immoral, nor idolaters, nor adulterers, nor sexual perverts, nor thieves, nor the greedy, nor drunkards, nor revilers, nor robbers will inherit the kingdom of God.*
>
> — I CORINTHIANS 6:9

THE CAR PHONE RINGS, doesn't really ring because nothing rings anymore. Instead, it chirps like an electronic grasshopper. Saul Messer knows this sound well. In his sock drawer at home he has five cellular phones, each of a different size and capability, all outdated. I mean, what are you meant to do with these hi-tech gizmos? You can't just throw them away, too expensive for that, and it's tough to hand them off to friends as gifts. (Friends get pissed at the assumption that your has-beens are their will-bes.) Maybe give one to your daughter, but she's only nine and you don't want to spoil her. Nothing worse than jappy kids yapping away like little adults. *Oh, darling! Really? That's staggering!* No joke, kids today talk like that. It's gotten to the point where you don't fear X-rated language anymore— fuck and shit would be a relief—but cringe with shame at *ciao,* at *fabulous,* at *no-can-do.* I swear, your daughter has a

mouth like a Gabor sister. So what do you do with your old
cell phones? Do you give them to your housekeeper, to your
gardener? "Here you go, a little something, you know, for a
job well done." Nope, that's out of the question, too imperi-
alistic for a good democrat like you. Maybe resell them—
always an option—but how do you go about doing that? A
pawn shop? A secondhand store? Can you imagine driving
up in your Porsche and unloading a box of old electronic
gear? There's a man who knows the meaning of a buck,
that's what they'll say the second you leave the place. Trust
me. They'd probably speculate that you're some down-and-
out movie Jew, which you are, but hell, you're much more
than just another down-and-out movie Jew. That's the short
division of your life, and right now you're as complicated as
differential calculus. So what do you do with that Motorola
Micro T.A.C Lite? Nothing you can do but slip it next to the
Corola SX-50, the Corola 7 series, the Centaur, and the
Motorola Por-Cell. Dead technology laid to rest next to a
pair of cashmere socks.

Saul lets the car phone chirp away. He strokes its black
plastic shell and tries to do some sort of Carnac routine.
*You'll never work in this town again! And may fleas infest
the underwear of your father's lover.* (Didn't Johnny Carson
have a great way of opening up those envelopes; he'd slice
through the top, then blow to puff out the innards, all that
self-important posturing for a corny joke. And don't you
sometimes find yourself opening up your mail with the same
technique? It's inevitable. Stuff like that imprints on your
brain, like theme music and holiday good cheer and remarks
on the mostly unchanging weather; like kissing your wife
hello and good-bye, good night and good morning; like the
endless best wishes and compliments and regards and
respects to people you know and barely know, your life a
history of innocuous greetings, your day-to-day determined
with less and less intention.) But Saul doesn't bother with

actually answering these calls. No point. It's all the same. Blah blah blah. And it's been ringing nonstop for the last seven hours. But early on, in the beginning, during those first few hours of driving (heading east to go west, if you know what I mean), he picked up the phone. It's a habit, a trained response in Pavlov Angeles. "Saul, where are you?" his annoyed secretary asked him. "You can't do this."

"Stop calling," he said.

"Saul, you're a big boy, act like one."

"Waaaaaaaa!"

And his wife had dialed him up a couple of times. Anna with that lazy French accent and sloped continental body; she defies gravity. There's also a certain Asian quality to her skin and cheekbones, her long black hair, her almond eyes. Exotic is the word and exotic ages well—at forty-three she still looks good, model good, yummy good, and there's a joke around town that she must bathe in the blood of virgins. In other words, her preserved beauty is almost B-movie creepy. But what can you do about genes? Nothing. Sure, you can take care of yourself—stay out of the sun, eat the right foods, don't drink too much booze—but so much depends on your particular batch of deoxyribonucleic acid. In terms of the complexities of Anna's personality, ice queen will do. Anyway, on the phone she said, "You can't run away, darling," with her usual existential nonchalance. To Saul, the whole thing should've sounded more histrionic à la a loved one trying to coax a gun-toting maniac into releasing his hostages. But no, she spoke calmly, almost bored, as if such desperate behavior was nothing new to the Gallically challenged. When you get down to it—and this is a thought Saul has maybe once a day—he should've married another Jew, someone with an equally heavy Levantine face that aged with each passing second. Instead, he fell for a *chic*sa— his mother's word—a boy toy goy. "It's not worth it," his wife told him.

"What?"

"Just come home."

"I will."

"Now."

He said, "At some point," and then he hung up, didn't really hang up—those days of cradle-slamming good-byes are over—no, he just pushed the "end" button. Not very satisfying. Some irate people, like the studio chief, toss their cellulars across the room, smashing them against the wall for effect. Shrapnel explodes; the oak paneling is given a half-moon nick. Saul had recently watched this display and immediately tallied the expense, but he couldn't deny the power of that particular production value. It certainly sent a fright through his spine. A real grabber. Maybe that's what you do with old cell phones and computers: you wait for that right moment—say it's a meeting of scriptwriters and you think their script is complete crap—and you pick up the moldy PC you've dragged out of the closet and you make a show of throwing it out the window. Bombs away! That'll get the idea across. A nice little drama for those geeky word-smiths.

"Daddy, I'm scared. Please come home," that's what his daughter was saying an hour ago. Saul is sure some rehearsal was involved. He could imagine his wife coaching her, running lines back and forth until Missy had it down cold. She's a hammy kid, an atavist of some forgotten vaudevillian Messer. Dance lessons: tap, jazz, ballet; voice lessons; something called poise, pronunciation, and polish. If she sees a piano she'll insist on singing her signature song, "Memory." Even at a packed restaurant, she'll beg and plead until you've got to give in. "This is a number that's dear to my heart," she'll tell her makeshift audience. And the scary thing is that a lot of people think it's the most adorable thing. "We miss you terribly," she said amid the bacon crackle of spotty coverage. "Really. We'll always love you the way you are. No matter." And it was almost enough to make Saul slam on the brakes and turn the Porsche around. But he didn't. Like most stunts he admired the mastery, the pyrotechnics, the precision, but within the explosions he always saw a thick bottom line of expenditure. Anna had probably promised Missy something, maybe a suede jacket with frills, or possibly a dog. There's always incessant talk about a dog. I swear, you can make a nine-year-old eat shit if you promise her a dog.

Saul downshifts the Porsche and kicks the RPM needle into the 5 X 1000 section of the tachometer. The car is speeding thirty miles over the posted speed limit, but it's dark out, well into the middle of the night, and speed slips into the relative ease of evening without the blur of things, of fields of suburbs turning into expanse of desert turning into mountains; instead, there's only that crescent of lit blacktop. And when Saul finds himself on a long stretch of empty road, he steers into the middle of the highway and pretends that this car is some great beast with glowing eyes and that the broken yellow lines are helpless creatures trapped in the mailroom of the evolutionary chain.

I KNOW this is terrible but this is the way Saul thinks about movie disasters: they're like Nazi death camps of World War II and their names are enough to make your blood cold: *Cleopatra* . . . Dachau; *Heaven's Gate* . . . Auschwitz; *Ishtar* . . . Treblinka; *Howard the Duck* . . . Lublin; *Hudson Hawk* . . . Buchenwald. Whole studios nearly destroyed, careers forever lost, all because of one lousy picture, and a picture that once looked so good, a picture people were banking on, a picture earmarked for a big summer release, a picture with can't-miss stars, a real boffo. How can you live in a universe like that, where talent doesn't mean shit, where a five-million-dollar movie can gross a hundred million and a hundred-million movie can gross five million, where six million Jews can be sent to a systematic slaughter, grandparents and aunts and uncles, a whole swath of cousins, a family tree treated like a pile of leaves? And no one learns diddly. Check out the news, the same stuff is happening over and over again (*Waterworld* . . . Rwanda), and while you know enough not to believe in progress, you still want to believe in growth, in maturity; you want to stop jacking off to that *Playboy*; you want to stay faithful to your wife, your parents, your religion; you want your daughter to love you always and you want to die wise and beloved even though when you get down to it you don't want to die at all. Never.

Saul turns up the music. At night the CD player casts an eerie red light, like Vegas from thirty miles out. And when Saul passed Vegas a few hours ago, the hotels pulsating from the highway, the shows in their second set, he thought about stopping and staying at the MGM Grand and maybe blowing a few thousand at the tables and getting blown for a few hundred. People would understand; they'd laugh and shake their heads and roll their eyes. So Hollywood. But Saul didn't turn off at any of the half dozen exits. Nope. He kept going north on Interstate 15, just a single highway creeping up like America's varicose vein. Is this a midlife crisis? Is it something that cheap, all these shitty feelings? Saul hopes it's not that clichéd. But there are moments, on the road, where all the cars seem to be filled with men who look like him, men on their way to a caucus of desperate behavior. So plow forward, you lemmings, to the edge of your actions! The sound-track music swells with violins—you can't believe the cost that goes into incidental music—and within the DEFCON Denon glow, Saul grips the leather handle of the emergency brake and mutters, "Drive, drive drive."

AT St. George, Utah time leaps forward an hour into Mountain Time (a phrase that makes you think of mewly John

Denver sitting atop a precipice and singing about the virtues of clean Rocky living). In an instant it's no longer late on Thursday night but early on Friday morning. Saul immediately fiddles his watch's hour hand. How easy it is to be a time traveler, to hurtle through time, to collect time and then to give it away. That's why the Concorde from London is such a kick. Pick up and leave and arrive before you left. How often can you get that? A real-life flashback.

10:48 A.M. *Thursday.*

In his office, a corner office, Saul says, "Fuck me," and then pauses for a second or two and says, "Fuck fuck." When upset, he relies on that word like a baby relies on a pacifier.

"What?"

"You heard me. Fuck me. Fuck me, fuck me, fuck me. Have you seen this?" He waves the *Variety* in front of his secretary's face. "Have you seen this fucking hatchet job? It's insane." Saul squeezes the bottle of Evian hard enough so that its ribbed plastic pops. Water shoots out and wets the splint on his broken middle finger, wets his shirt, wets the blotter on his desk.

"I'll get you a towel," the secretary says.

"Fuck that; have you seen this?" He tosses the paper—it flutters in sections, a failed flying machine.

"Yes, I have."

Saul rolls up his sleeves. He wants to look intimidating, powerful, young—Christ, does he want to look young, mid-thirties instead of mid-forties, just a lousy ten years!—so his trainer has been working on his arms, giving them corporate buff. "I thought this reporter was a friend," Saul says. "You know, in pocket."

"He has been."

"I tell you, the fucking new morality of this world. Everyone's Serpico. Or at least everyone thinks they're Serpico. Serpico's cool. Blow the lid off. Yeah, that's it. The last good guy. The last honest man in America. The fucking whistle-blower to the corrupted soul. So turn colors. Rip off that mask. Reveal the real you. Here I am to save the day! While all this time the old you was just a spy to this vileness you once loved. Taking notes while you dutifully take the perks. Give me a break! I mean, it's just a movie. Am I right, Cloris? It's just a fucking movie. And a historical movie at that. It's not the downfall. This isn't the lead in the pipes. A movie. It's just a movie. Entertainment. Not worthy of this Woodward-and-Bernstein approach."

The secretary, uncertain at what to do, picks up a tray of bagels and Danishes and offers him something called a Morning Delight. "They're wonderful," she says.

11:47 A.M. *Thursday.*

After numerous phone calls—the studio chief, reporters, wife—a knock on the door and his assistant walks in holding a wrapped package under her beautiful bare arm. "We have it," she says.

"Has anyone seen it?" His hand instinctively hides his broken finger, the surgical tape a white flag of surrender.

"No, no one has. This isn't airing for a week. I have a friend."

"Good work."

She unwraps the brown paper and walks to the TV— well, actually she struts, she's a strutter, ass wiggling like it's cleaning a windshield at one of those nudie car washes. She inserts the tape, pushes it ever so gently until the black tongue is pulled within the machine. Yes, this is quite a performance. And yes, Saul has slept with her. I mean, it's on your mind, don't deny it. Men want to fuck her and women want to hate her, that's the Eszterhasian coverage on her first impression. So yes, they had a one-night stand, about a week ago. You see, he was feeling down from everything, failure looming overhead in Cuban-missile-crisis fashion: any day, the bomb would drop. There was no escaping it, his lot held in celluloid. And here was this attractive woman, and smart, and willing, and young. When did twenty-four seem so young? When does that happen? Sure, fifteen, sixteen, seventeen, positively illegal; eighteen, nineteen, robbing the cradle; but how did the early twenties slip into something considered innocent and naive and pure? And that night, last Tuesday.

9:48 P.M. Last Tuesday.
"I love you."
"What?"
Saul looks down at her. They've barely begun. He's just slid inside of her and she's just done this thing with her legs, a thing he'd never seen or even thought about before, and a light—who knows where it comes from but it's magical: big fat atoms of light buzzing around like fireflies—seems to flow from her face, her skin, pores popping with paparazzi flare. Man-oh-man, it's head-rushing fireworks, and he says it again. "I love you."
She stops moving. "You love me?"
Saul pauses, thinks for a second (Does this mean divorce? Is this binding? Is this a bad thing to say?) and maintains his claim with a stout "Yes."
"You barely know me."
"True."
"Okay," she says, "you love me." And she turns him around with some sort of wrestling move and boom! she's on top of him and she's stretching backward and reaching behind to cradle his balls . . . whoops, not the balls, the asshole, her index finger circling the puckered ring. This is new to Saul, that area strictly off limits in matters sexual, even though his wife is European and he's heard things. But assholes, bungs, rectums, poopers, anuses (what is the right

word? they all sound awful) have never entered his realm of
bedroom activities. What if you like it too much? What does
that mean? Do you suddenly have to reevaluate who you
are? I mean, of course not, you're straight and that's never
been one of the issues you've lumbered under, but still, this
was feeling good, and yow! she eases her index finger into
you, stopping at the first knuckle. Instinctively, your back
arches up (it just does) and she pinches her knees against
your ribs. Is this fun? It's hard to tell. To say this is the first
time Saul has cheated on his wife would be a lie. But he's a
decent husband, and besides, he's answered quite a few
phone calls from mysterious men claiming to have the
wrong number. Such things happen in life, small affairs for
one night, possibly two, once for a month. But this is the
first time he's professed love. Why? Who knows? But sometimes you're falling, twisting from the ninth floor, a real Dar
Robinson stunt, and while you struggle through the air like
a moth caught in a pool, you hope love will inflate some airy
pillow. Does that make sense? Saul isn't sure, but since this
woman has her finger up his ass, he says it again.

"You are so beautiful. I really think I love you."

She stares up toward the ceiling, exposing a scar along
the bone of her chin. An accident as a kid? An abusive
boyfriend? Passing out in a bathroom? Saul wants to ask
but she's crunching through a workout, her face bundled
with concentration. She eases her finger to the second
knuckle. Saul feels a slight burning in a previously unknown
spot. And he thinks: Is this going to make me poop? Childhood suppositories dance in his head, memories of his
mother chasing him around the Brooklyn apartment while
he dodged her in constipated despair.

"Do it to me," she says.

"What?"

"Finger me."

"Huh?"

"My asshole." She stops moving long enough for Saul to satisfy her request. He finds the place in question and fulfills the desire. (He can't believe he's doing this.) It makes her shudder and she starts to rock with a brand-new vigor. "This kills me," she says.

"I love you."

"I'm going to come."

It must've been a four-minute performance, or at least close to it, and square in the middle of this gargantuan orgasm she withdraws her finger from Saul (my God! that leaves you with a sense of emptiness and regret) and starts feeling her own breasts—pinch pinch pinch—and this really puts her over the edge because she then throws herself backward and breaks Saul's finger.

11:50 A.M. *Thursday again.*

You shut your finger in the car door, that's your story. It was late and you were tired and you crawled into the front seat of the Porsche and whammo! blinding pain. The doctor bought it. So did the wife. Missy kissed the splint to make it better. But Saul wonders if the story holds water. I mean, can you really close your middle finger in a car door? Sure, if you try. But by accident? No way. Not just one finger. But nobody questioned him and this made Saul question everything. Easy alibis swirled within the worst injuries, lies transformed by agony.

The assistant turns on the TV and eases back toward Saul's desk, coyly leaning against the corner. Of course there are a couple of scenes left out of last Tuesday's encounter. On the cutting-room floor, you might say. There's the assistant's misreading Saul's cries of pain for cries of pleasure. It's a classic case of comedic misunderstanding, almost farcical. Imagine his screams—*Ahhhh!* or something along those lines—and her excited grinding—*Oh, yes, harder!* or words to that effect—and then, in a flash of resignation, he passes out. And after that there's the ride to the emergency room, the bandaging of the finger, the constant throbbing, but such images Saul would rather forget. The uncontrollable tears, the screaming, the nurse's coldness, the lonely drive home. Some people are not made to suffer; they are the first to die in hardship.

The assistant says, "You ready?"

Saul nods.

She pushes a button on the remote control and the screen flickers to two men, well-known film critics, one fat and one thin, their names dependent on each other as Abbot is dependent on Costello (unidentified here for reasons liable). Saul leans forward. Certainly, he's feeling tension, in the stomach, the lower half. Success is not a word recently associated with this man, though successes had popped up in his past, nice successes, well-regarded by the critics, nicely attended by the public, successes that had been nominated for awards but didn't win. But his last success was six years ago and it was barely a success. Since then, duds, four duds in a row, and now, with this newest release, all signs prophesize a big disaster. The endless test screenings pointed to elements too large to fix: *The bad teeth are distracting! Such fake snow! Does it have to be so depressing? Why would I ever pay money to sit through this?!* I guess when you get down to it, a movie about the Donner Party isn't such a hot idea. Flesh-eating only works in horror flicks. And these days everyone is cynical about earnestness. (There was laughter in one screening when an exiled John Reed proclaimed to his family, "We will be together, I promise you. We will be together someday. Please remember that.") But the director was A-list, the screenwriter first-rate, the actors well-respected (one of them a teen idol searching for legitimacy), and Saul had secured a healthy budget from the studio. Problem was the budget didn't take into effect a freakishly warm winter, a broken leg, union troubles,

Native American protests, an addicted director of photography, and the crews' proximity to Reno. The budget swelled the same way a cartoon snowball rolling down a hill swells into a deadly boulder sucking up everything in its path. But right now a possible triumph might be snatched from the jaws of bad buzz, cinematic fate determined by a thumbs-up or a thumbs-down from these emperors of public taste.

With a push of a button the fat one and the thin one jerk from fast forward into real time. "Here we go," the assistant says.

11:57 A.M. *Thursday.*

They hated it. Two thumbs down, way down, to China down, the China Syndrome of bad movies, down, down, down until clear through to the other side of awful. The fat one actually called it "How the West Was Eaten." That's a bit harsh, isn't it? You can have an opinion but you don't have to be nasty about it. But do you know what really hurts? It's that Saul's just as gawky as these two film nerds: balding in an undignified manner, bad skin, an inability to catch or throw or hit. In high school he probably would've been friends with these guys, skipping class to go to movies, sitting toward the front so as not to see the couples making out during *Spartacus*. So this seems a betrayal of the worst kind, the brotherhood of awkward men destroyed for showbiz's sake. Why the abuse? Are we not mensches? Saul, never much of a student of the Torah, just quick with a Yiddish word or phrase, sits there and remembers celebrating Yom Kippur with his family, back in Canarsie, on Remsen Ave. He'd have to accept the apologies of the stronger boys who tormented him throughout the year, his father forcing forgiveness with a full heart, and twenty-five hours later, after the single note of the shofar, the regularly scheduled abuse would begin all over again. And then there was the fasting between the bookends of sundown, Saul sneaking food in the bathroom, Ziplocked cookies hidden in the toilet tank while the stories of the oral tradition were told. The sacrificing of the goats comes to mind: the one goat offered at the altar, the other goat released into the wilderness: "And Aaron shall lay both his hands upon the head of the live goat, and confess over him all the iniquities of the people of Israel, and all their transgressions, all their sins; and he shall put them upon the head of the goat, and send him away into the wilderness by the hand of a man who is in readiness." Funny what can pop into your head, thoughts with long beards and awful smells, draped in black, Hasidic simplicity now garbed in Hollywood cool.

The assistant stops the tape. The TV screen skips onto the color of a clear video sky. "Well," she says, drumming the remote against her thigh. "That doesn't really mean a thing. Look down the list of yearly top tens and you'll see thumbs down on more than half."

Saul nods.

"It'll open big."

And before she leaves, pausing at the door, her body half in and half out, hand flicking the doorknob so that the latch makes mechanical clicks, she asks, "Oh, how's your finger, by the way?" And she smiles—with playfulness or with ridicule, who can tell with a woman like that?

1:17 P.M. *Thursday.*

Saul sneaks out of the building. The fresh air doesn't feel so fresh or even much like air; it's more like breathing through a mixture of cotton candy and insulation. The people he recognizes give him pained smiles pretending that failure, in the grand scheme, isn't much of a tragedy. For example, you could lose a loved one. And at least you have your health. But screw that, you'd take cancer right now, HIV, a terrible maiming collision. At this moment, you'd gladly collapse on the caskets of your wife and daughter.

Just give me grosses! You can be a martyr—in fact, personal calamity would probably be good for you, a test of the human spirit—but professional ruin is not a role you want to be cast in. It all comes down to being active and passive (this is what your shrink says). You can't control misfortune, so there's a certain freedom to luxuriate in it. But the rest is a cowbell of responsibility: every time you move, you clatter.

The high-pitched tweet of a car alarm—bee-boop!—and Saul is in his Porsche and Saul is out the gate and Saul is going east. He leans back into the traffic and does what little steering he has to with his knees. Above him, a pigeon flies—circling? do pigeons circle?—while the midday light hits its wings with vulturous foreboding. Even birds act.

6:15 A.M. *Friday. Right now.*

The sun is rising to the left with the syrupy promise of Little Orphan Annie to bet your bottom dollar. (What was John Huston thinking, but at least he had emphysema as an excuse.) Saul, infinitely tired, drives twenty miles with each blink of his lids. Whoa! what happened there? A brief moment on the rumble strips, the sensation similar to a 5.3 on the Richter scale, and Saul is awake and gripping the steering wheel and jerking back into the middle of the road. That can give you a small heart attack. Luckily, the traffic is sparse. No one is out at this hour. Saul grabs the two-gallon bottle of Coke and takes a long sip. Disgusting. Warm and flat, the landscape's equivalent in carbonate. Where are the mountains anyway? Shouldn't this be the opening shot of *Bonanza?*

After Monida Pass, you enter Montana—The Last Best Place, Big Sky Country. Friends in Saul's business are buying ranches here left and right, sprinkling the sage with glitter. Property is no longer discussed in three-to-five-acre plots, swimming pools and tennis courts, ocean views. Now it's the lingo of spreads, ten thousand acres, five hundred head of cattle, a lake, a river, a mountain. Rugged individualism is held within land, and real estate agents can get it for you cheap. Just plop down a couple of million and you're a new pioneer with manifest destiny.

Saul perks up a bit. He's done it. This was the goal. Montana by car. Sixteen hours ago it actually made sense, but like much impetuous behavior, it's in jeopardy of turning foolish. So where do you go now? The wing-and-a-prayer structure is showing signs of a weak third act. Nothing worse. You can't leave them bored, checking their watches, scraping the bottom of the popcorn barrel. That kills word of mouth. Always better to end with a bang. The test audience that sits in Saul's synapticplex wonders if there's a point to this journey. *Too aimless, not much action.* Hell, they can't even decide if the protagonist is a sympathetic character. *An adulterous movie producer. A rich Hollywood Jew. A self-involved egoist.* He's simply not likable, not interesting, not good entertainment value, not worth the price of admission. And what can you do to save yourself? Nothing. No reedits. No reshoots. Just rush it straight to video and hope nobody notices. Saul feels the unique tingle of an anxiety attack—it starts with prickly flashes, like being beamed up in *Star Trek,* except the *Enterprise* is cold and empty and boldly going nowhere.

Up ahead, the emerald of a road sign—"Dillon, 75 miles"—and the first thing that pops into mind is the actor Matt Dillon playing the lawman Matt Dillon in a movie adapted from the TV show. This high concept puts Saul at ease, temporarily.

OUT OF THE blue and with soundless pursuit, the flashing red of a Montana State Trooper appears in the Porsche's rearview mirror. Saul, exhausted yet determined, doesn't notice the approaching lights—he only has nine more miles left until Dillon, then he'll stop and have breakfast and maybe take a nap and think about things. "Reevaluate" is the word he's looking for, but at this moment he can't find any word over three syllables long.

After a minute of being ignored, the siren wails.

"Shit." Where did that come from? No billboards to hide behind, no trees or blind turns; everything is within sight. Saul clicks on his hazards—a blatant attempt at ingratiating himself with the law—and eases onto the shoulder, decelerating gradually and with professional care. His adrenaline, on hold for the last ten hours, now cuts loose with a torrent of epinephrine. Palms begin to sweat. Throat fills with saliva. And a sense of a greater guilt washes away any chance of presumed innocence.

A trooper with the prerequisite sharp hat and mirrored sunglasses and mustache ambles up to Saul's window, his left hand casual on the butt of his revolver. "Hi there," he says. His relaxed manner is threatening in a Southern way: corrupt affability.

"Hi."

"License and registration."

"Here you go." Saul hands over his documentation. "For some reason, I thought there wasn't a speed limit in Montana. Read it in the paper or something."

The trooper smiles. "That isn't quite true. It's discretionary. If it's open road and no traffic, I'm not going to stop you unless you're being a real idiot. But in other circumstances I might pull you over for going seventy. Truth is, I can decide anything I want."

"Oh."

"You been driving long, Mr. Messer?"

"Since I was a kid."

"I mean recently, Mr. Messer."

"Oh, I see. Yes, all the way from California."

"Where you going in Montana?"

Saul sees a possible opening. "Well, I'm not sure," he says. "I'm kind of here to scout locations for a project. I'm in the movies, business side, you see, and I'm trying to find a nice town, a charming town, a town that has a certain flavor to it. Do you know any?" This schmooze often works, sometimes getting him the best hotel rooms at half price.

"Anaconda's nice. Do you have any drugs in the car, Mr. Messer?"

"No. Nothing."

"Any weapons?"

"No."

"What happened to your finger?"

"Broke it. Slammed it in a door."

"Ouch! Gotta hurt. Do you know why I stopped you, Mr. Messer?"

"Not really."

"You were going forty-five miles per hour in the left lane. That's a bit slow for this highway. Can be dangerous to other vehicles. We do have a minimum speed in this state."

Saul nods. "I guess I'm tired," he says.

"You look it." The trooper straightens, pulling himself up by the belt. "I'm going to go and run your name through the computer, see what comes up, then I'll come back and tell you what's going on. Okay?"

"Sounds good."

The trooper leaves, and Saul watches him in the rearview mirror: in the front seat of the squad car, head down, hands typing, eyes reading. The computer. What's being spat up onto the screen? Maybe a few parking tickets, speeding violations, a DUI from twelve years ago, that's about it. Nevertheless, Saul grows worried, and the longer he waits—ticktock ticktock ticktock—the more he becomes convinced that something is in fact wrong. Has the registration expired? Have all the fines been paid? Is there an outstanding debt? Has your wife filed a missing person report?

Did the studio discover your slight history of embezzle-
ment? Is screwing your assistant a form of sexual harass-
ment? Does an incidental erection while playing horsey
with your daughter warrant an arrest for incest? Can
spousal abuse be declared for long silences, for under-the-
breath muttering, for blatant acts of narcissism? And then
what about all of those sacred laws, the laws of your people, the halakah—shit, you are the Dillinger of Judaism.

The trooper steps out of his car, a clipboard in hand.
Saul slowly pedals in the clutch—it creaks like a haunted
door. The trooper drops something, a pen, and he bends
down to pick it up. Saul pinches the key in the ignition—the
fish key chain, a gift from his daughter, dangles back and
forth. The trooper is at the window, and he says, "Okay,
Mr. Messer," but before he can say another word, Saul has
the car started and he guns the engine—a little too quick on
the clutch—and just barely catches the gear. He peels out.
Unfortunately, there's no gravel to kick up, but soon the
Porsche is climbing past a hundred miles per hour and Saul
is weaving in and out of the now present morning traffic,
his eyes searching the rearview mirror for any signs of the
fuzz.

FOUR minutes later, the car phone chirps, and Saul instinctively answers.

"Yeah," he says.

"Mr. Messer?"

"Speaking." Saul doesn't recognize the voice; it's too
calm.

"This is Trooper DeKirk, the trooper you just fled."

Saul freezes—first thought: how did he get this number?—then he says, "Yes, officer." Rather lame for a fugitive.

"Well, Mr. Messer, I'll tell you what, a rookie would get
a real kick out of you. Yep, he would. This is some good
action, Porsche and all, but I'm a bit old for this high-speed
crap. You're in entertainment, right? That's what you said."

"Yes."

"You know what show I just loved? *The Andy Griffith Show.* That was my favorite."

"I'm involved with film, not TV."

"Whatever. All I'm saying is that I like to bring a little of that Mayberry style to the troopers. You know, a country approach. I sing, too. Go to schools and stuff. Safety classes. So I really don't want to do some crazy shit out of *Bullitt* right now. I'm not the type. Hell, I used to be, but not now. And I'm sure you're not the type. And you don't want to become a first-time felon. Believe me, Mr. Messer. So why don't you pull over and I'll be there pretty soon to give you a warning for driving too slow. Maybe we'll talk for a bit, the way Andy used to talk to Otis."

"I'm not a drunk."

"I know that, Mr. Messer. I was just saying we could talk. But do me a favor and pull over before I get frustrated. This is silly. A black Porsche in Montana sticks out."

There's an exit for Dillon, and Saul slows down and puts on his blinker and takes the curve of the ramp with geometrical precision. A sign points toward a business loop.

"Mr. Messer, you there?"

Saul thinks about the new wave of popular pulp-trash flicks, and he almost shouts, *Come and get me, you dirty copper,* but instead simply says "Yes" before pushing the "end" button.

JOLLY Pack Rat Used Motors is strung with out-of-season Christmas lights, a canopy of tacky color above the cars, the trailer office outlined like a bejeweled box of myrrh. Too bad the morning sun has washed out this effect. Saul parks between a Ford Bronco and a Chevy Wrangler. Stepping away, gauging its visibility from the main drag, Saul wonders how he ever managed to fit into such a car. It's so small you'd think you'd be able to slip it in your pocket. Saul imagines a child's hand pushing the matchbox Porsche along a carpet, the roar of the motor nothing more than a labial sound effect.

The sign on the door says "Closed," but through the window a man can be seen reading the newspaper, drinking coffee, eating a glazed doughnut. Saul knocks.

"One second." And after a few moments of shuffling, the door opens. The man, a large guy who looks more like a coal miner than a salesman, smiles and says, "Want some coffee?"

"What?"

"Coffee, I got a pot."

"That'd be great."

The man disappears into the trailer—Saul notices an unmade cot in the corner and a few moving boxes with clothes spilling over the sides. He comes back and hands Saul an Elks Club mug and says, "Shall we take a little walk around? My name's Jolly. Pack Rat's just one of those war nicknames, you know, stuff to make you sound tougher. Funny thing's Jolly's a nickname too, a junior high thing, you know, *get your jollies off*. Well, that was me. Whew! those were the days, weren't they? Even in Montana. But when I got into this business I thought I'd just combine the two because I'll tell you what, in the end, when all the chips are cashed in, I'm more Jolly than Fred and I'm more Pack Rat than McGlynn." While speaking, Jolly has led Saul straight to the Porsche. "Now to get to business: you selling or buying?"

"Both."

"I see, a little trade." Jolly sits on the hood of the car—the tires flatten a bit—and he rocks up and down. Something squeaks. "Pretty warm, you been driving from California?"

"Yes."

"You know what—now what's your name?"

"It's Stretch. Stretch Larson." Saul is extremely satisfied with his quick thinking.

"Stretch? Okay. Sure. You really should be here at night,

Stretch, with the lights, I mean, because this place is . . . sublime." He leans back against the windshield, arms crossing behind his neck. "I tell you what, Stretch, I love the mix of winter darkness and daylight savings. That's as good as it gets. Look forward to it. To me, summer's dead."

"Listen, Jolly, I'm in a hurry."

"I can tell."

"And I'm willing to give you a pretty propitious deal."

"Once again, Stretch, I can tell." Jolly rolls over on his side. "Propitious. That's a good word. Propitious. Nice in the mouth. Of late, things haven't been so propitious for me. Very unpropitious, in fact. Wife and I are at war, and she's not abiding any Geneva Convention." Saul points to his watch, hoping to cut short this back-story spiel, but Jolly keeps on talking. "You know what, Stretch? You know what I've been thinking? In Vietnam I was never a POW, but I would've been a good one. Like Bill Holden in *The Bridge on the River Kwai*. Or *King Rat*. Even the crap that went down in *The Deer Hunter*. But fuck all, I never got caught, not when it would've meant something to me, and now I'll never find out what's the worst I can live with, you know, the deepest depths, where stars are the only virtue. Seems important to me, more important than a job skill."

Inside the Porsche, the car phone chirps.

"You got a call."

Saul steps forward. "I'm going to let it ring. In fact—" He opens the door, reaches down and rips out the car phone, wires and all. It surrenders with surprising ease. He hands over the plastic clump to Jolly. "Let's cut to the chase, shall we? I'll do a straight trade, the red Dodge Ram over there for the Porsche. But let me tell you what I don't have. I don't have a license, a registration, title. Can we work around those issues?"

"I think so." Jolly slides off the hood and onto his feet. "That was pretty cool, what you did," he says.

"I'm also going to need Montana plates for the Ram."

"I'll hunt you up a pair."

"And I'd appreciate it if you held off from taking the Porsche out for a spin. Just for a couple of days. It's not stolen, I promise you that."

"No big deal." Jolly shakes his head, a baffled expression on his face. "You don't look like an outlaw."

And before reaching into the Porsche for his briefcase, Saul can't resist the perfect comeback. "Looks," he says, "can be deceiving."

Jolly kicks the dirt. "Jesus. I fed you that line."

PARKING IN the Kmart, the cars in their neat rows, Saul is tempted to throw the truck into four-wheel drive and charge over the compacts and subcompacts. Pancake them! You could do it. In first gear this rig feels like a tank. And you certainly get a different perspective from this height, a feeling of invincibility, a monster truck ego where only the most extreme forms of nature can slow you down.

The Ram takes up two spaces. Saul climbs down—there's an actual step—and walks inside the store. Never been in this kind of place before. It's huge, a warehouse of middle-class value, the customers strictly an action-movie crowd. Signs hang from the ceiling—Lingerie, Candy, Hardware—swinging in the draft like executed bandits. Saul grabs a cart and serpentines toward the Men's Department, where he rifles through racks of clothes, grabbing an assortment of plaid shirts, jeans, an eight-pack of white socks, a denim jacket, a hat—this is kind of enjoyable. How about some heavy gloves and a University of Montana sweatshirt and a pair of steel-toed boots and a hunting knife and a toolbox, and while in the Personal Care aisle, why not pick up a bottle of Brute cologne and Old Spice deodorant and Vitalis and a Reach toothbrush with a scoliotic curve. By the time Saul wheels to the register, the cart is brimming with the makings of a new person.

The cashier, a young woman tragically close to being pretty, sweeps the items over the scanner—beep!—and buries them in plastic bags. When four bags are packed and redeposited in the cart, she says, "That'll be $198.37."

Saul counts the money straight into her hand, amazed at how cheap everything is. And the cashier becomes giddy with the growing pile, as if, in some alternate universe, this cash belongs to her.

AFTER pumping gas—that dirty self-service makes you feel tough, to the point where you want to check the oil and envision mechanic expertise in a dipstick—Saul changes clothes in the Mobil rest room. The new duds are tight and scratchy and militantly out of fashion; the old designer suit is thrown into a dumpster. Saul pulls the yellow CAT hat tight to his head and wipes his hands against his shirt. Let's get a move on. And as he walks to the truck, he almost expects to hear the shout of some celestial Everyone-in-come-free, telling him the game is over. Time to go home for lunch. But Saul keeps playing. The other game is over. And he'll never eat lunch in that town again. Nope.

So, on to Anaconda, the definition of boom and bust held within the dead monuments of smelter towers, toxic mines, and immense pits (plus you've got to like the name: not only a huge South American snake, but also a type of poker game where each player is dealt seven cards, discards two, then plays the remaining five, flipping over one after each round of betting, the truth revealed in increments). Years ago, there was so much copper in these hills that it was nicknamed Copperopolis, but production has slowed, and more and more people try to get by with poker. Saul tunes into a country station, and finds himself saying amen to Waylon Jennings. Yes, yes, amen.

A FEW hours later Saul corrals the Ram in front of Sladich's Bar. What a surprise to see a name like this out west. Inside, he half expects cowboy rabbis huddled over the bar, the Torah unscrolled the entire length. Not too far from the truth. Alcohol can have the power of the Pentateuch. Genesis . . . Jim Beam. And certainly the debate is lively even though everyone makes the same point: *All down the shitter, the whole kit and caboodle!* These muttering men notice Saul's arrival but they don't stare for more than a second. The sole woman, her eyelashes so lacquered they practically crackle, has her arms around two geezers. They should be singing some bawdy song, the way they rock back and forth, but they don't seem to have the memory for the lyrics. Saul moseys to the bar. The amount of smoke is amazing, ashtrays blooming with spent cigarettes, and the floor is covered with the crushed exoskeletons of peanuts. But this adds to the unmistakable flavor of the West. In Disneyland, these people would be mechanical, drinking their whiskey, telling their pre-taped stories, only their outfits would be different: ten-gallon hats, chaps, holstered Colts, and maybe a player piano instead of a jukebox. Saul scoots onto a stool and—what the hell—shouts. "Drinks on the house."

The bartender pokes his head up. "What the fuck?" he says.

"Drinks all around. On me, I guess. Drinks on me."

"Damn right," the bartender says. He goes about filling and refilling glasses, handing out beer. "And what do you want, Rockefeller?"

"A whiskey. Make it a double." Saul, nervous at the prospect of hard liquor, fiddles his bulky gold Rolex, close to ten thousand dollars on his wrist. Oh shit! Does everyone notice? I mean, you don't wear flashy jewelry—and that always seemed to be a sign of great restraint—but in here, your working-class conversion might be blown by precision timing. Saul slips off the watch; maybe he'll pawn it later.

The bartender pushes the whiskey forward. Saul picks up the drink, pauses, tries not to smell the high-octane fumes, smiles, slams back the shot (please, whatever you do, don't puke) and raps the empty glass against the counter. Eye ducts tear. Salivary glands flood. Everything threatens to liquefy, to overflow, but the levee holds and the booze recedes. Whew! An apple-juice chaser would be nice, something acidic to cut the aftertaste, but the bartender, without even asking, pours a refill.

"Oh, great," Saul says, defeated by charity. "I tell you what, give everyone a shot of their choice. I'm paying."

"You just bought a round."

"Well, I'm buying again." Saul bends over and sips off the amber meniscus (if only whiskey were more like wine). But the hard living of this second drink is a touch easier to stomach. He glances about the bar, disappointed at the initial public reaction to his generosity—nobody moves, nobody says thank you, nobody appreciates the money spent—but eventually, in collective slow motion, a dirty dozen surrounds this patron of the patrons.

"You feeling good?" one of them asks. He has a deposit of spittle on his lower lip, a small dot which conjoins to the upper lip every time he talks. "Must be feeling mighty fucking good, I'd say."

"I guess," Saul answers. "Though we're all miserable."

"I hear you."

Another person hobbles over with a severe limp—this is a town of limps, from logging accidents to motorcycle crashes to birth defects as a result of mining techniques, and the sidewalk often resembles a hospital hallway. He pats Saul on the shoulder. "I tell you the 'Auld Lang Syne' is playing today. Heard it when I woke. Guy Lombardo conducting in my head, clear as a bell." His words are not so much spoken as distilled.

Saul nods. "We might walk in newness of life."

"That's right."

Someone yells out, "Where you from?"

"Who the hell knows anymore?" Saul says.

A cluck of agreement. "Fucking said it, you did."

"What's the name?" the same someone yells out again.

"What does it matter? My people don't know me."

"You said it."

Saul looks over the crowd and tells them, "We are members of one another." And he pulls out his Italian-leather wallet and slaps down his second-to-last hundred-dollar bill. "Let's drink on Mr. Franklin's bill. I know he won't mind."

And yes, people cheer, and yes, people practically lift Saul onto their shoulders, as if he were a beloved coach on a forever losing team. "Good on you!" they say, their strength made perfect in weakness.

AN empty wallet later and everyone is second-stage drunk and everyone is in cars and everyone is driving to someone's house—it belongs to the quiet guy who stayed at the end of the bar, the guy who drank the free drinks without saying so much as a "Thanks" until he picked himself off the stool and said, "Party at my place." Saul hauls a cargo of men and loose bottles, each rolling with every turn, and next to him, in the front seat, sits a young man called Digger.

"Shit," Digger says, "I've always read about the mysterious stranger, ever since *Shane* in the sixth grade. Guess I've been waiting for him to show up, it seems at least. Can screw with your head, though. Things'll change, that's what you think, things'll change without lifting a goddamn finger. That's the problem with the whole country, I suppose."

"Alan Ladd," Saul mutters.

Digger cracks his knuckles against his chin. "So, mister," he says, "where you staying in Anaconda?"

"Don't know."

"My mom and I have an extra room. Could stay there, that is if you want."

"Maybe."

"Do you smoke grass?"

"Not right now."

"Okay. But if you want, just say 'Open sesame.' I also got some crystal meth if that's of interest."

The procession takes a left onto a "No Trespassing" dirt road and continues for another mile, along scrub, until it arrives at an old homesteading shack. This place is battered, a corner of the tin roof pared back, the porch sagging, but it still seems inhabitable. Curtains are in the windows; posies in the window boxes. The cars park in a haphazard fashion, and people stumble from their splayed wings. Everyone is unhappy with the brightness of the afternoon sun. Otherwise, there is a jubilance.

"Before we get to drinking, I wanted to have some fun." The host pops his trunk, reaches in and grabs gun after gun, all different sizes and different types: pistols, rifles, shotguns, assault weapons, a high-tension crossbow. Saul is amazed. It's like being at the circus and watching the clowns pile out of that tiny Volkswagen.

"All right!"

"There you go!"

"Whose place is this?" Saul asks.

The host says, "Mine," and then hands him an AK-47. Fully loaded, you just have to point and pull and light things up. "That's it, buddy. Blow the shit out of the old inheritance."

Saul slips his finger through the trigger guard; his splinted middle finger sticks out in a Fuck You kind of way. "Anyone in the house?" he asks.

"God no. Think I'm crazy? Just let her rip."

Saul aims down the barrel. What to shoot at? The window? In the movies all gunplay happens through windows, the shattering glass, the husband pushing his wife and child to the floor, the desperate crawling toward the .45 on the coffee table. Death only comes through the window. Or the door. Saul sights onto the weather-worn door. Often the secondary character gets it like this, answering the bell and kack! Saul fires. The noise is instant echo, the recoil bruising, but the result isn't nearly as impressive: a bloom of dust and a small hole. That's it. The smell of pyrocellulose enters his nose. Saul, a staunch gun-control advocate, expected more from such violence.

"You got to lean on it. Let it loose."

"Remember the fucking Alamo!"

"Porkchop Hill!"

Digger instructs, "Keep your finger down. Full fucking auto."

Without aiming this time, Saul empties the clip in a flurry of gunfire. This is more like it. The repetitious noise—kacka!kacka!kacka!—the shaking kick, the flash of expelled shell casings, the incidental warmth of the muzzle, all of this slowly melts your insides until the only thing that remains is the beat of your heart. It's like being underwater, in your pool, lungs ready for air, but you wait, you push yourself for no reason, just inches from the surface, waiting.

"You fucking killer!"

Saul, ammo spent, is given another banana clip and is shown how to eject and insert. It's very easy. He prepares to let loose again, the honored guest to this destruction, but down the road he notices a sheriff's patrol car approaching with a tail of dust. Shit! The gig is up. The state patrol's APB must've been picked up by the local law enforcement. Saul snuggles the stock of the AK-47 under his armpit. This is it. He squeezes the handgrip. The car stops. Surrender or go out in a blaze of glory. The engine shuts down. A fresh silence possesses all things. The sheriff staggers out, gravy stains on his untucked shirt, his belt mysteriously undone. Every step forward is accompanied by a step sideways. "Howdy, boys," he manages to say.

"Hey there, Willie."

The sheriff unholsters his gun and—boom! boom! boom! what the hell is that? a .357 Magnum?—fires. Saul flinches. Explosions wisp from the chimney; chunks of brick rain down on tin. "Roger be here soon with the flamethrower," the sheriff shouts.

"Super."

And now everyone is holding a gun, some holding two, and a massive volley cracks through the valley, and a renewed Saul joins the enfilade—wood splinters, glass breaks, curtains drift, posies shred into confetti—and as he blasts away, Saul imagines wave after wave of an attacking public, a persecuting public, their bodies falling to the ground, bleeding and injured, but there are more behind them, an endless charge from that front door, each person getting closer and closer, and your ammunition is running low, and your chances are slim, but at least you'll die a hero.

Girl with
Large Foot
Jumping Rope

My KID MAKES A controlled slide downstairs and stops in between me and the TV. He's a funny kid. People say he looks a lot like Becky—the slim nose, the oval mouth, the curly blond hair, while my hair is straight and black like a well-groomed Indian—but every time I look at him I see my eyes and my chin and I know that this is my boy. "Hey, Sport," I say. I call him Sport. It makes me *feel* like a father. "What's up, Sport?"

He doesn't say a word, simply stands there, Pledge-of-Allegiance straight. He's seven years old and short for his age—I guess it's a real issue at school, you know, with all the teasing, all the stupid names—and he does this crazy thing with his lips when he's upset, kind of curls them like a disgusted Frenchman. He's doing that now. "Everything all right, Sport?" I say.

He nods without conviction.

Then I glance down and notice his feet, his socks, really, those white athletic socks that kids wear all the time. Tube socks, we used to call them. Anyway, these socks are soaking wet, so are the cuffs of his pants. He looks as if he's been dancing in some fountain in Paris.

"What's up, Josh?" I say, dropping Sport and putting a little sternness in my voice, the you-can-tell-me sort of voice, the voice of the good cop. Becky is the bad cop.

It comes out in one burst, and since he's an emotional boy, he starts to cry. I can't understand a word the poor guy says, but whatever it is, it breaks my heart. I lean down and take him in my arms and rub the back of his neck and whisper in his ear, "It's all right, it's all right," even though I have no idea what he's done. But he's a pretty earnest kid with this incredible sense of justice, like he's a representative from the UN. I put him on my lap, and he curls in under my armpit. And Jesus, I almost get weepy. If the phone rang right now, I'd just let it ring.

"I'm sorry, Dad," Josh says after he's mostly controlled himself. He wipes at his eyes and nose with the sleeve of his shirt. But when he breathes, his body shudders. "I just, it just happened," he says.

I brush aside some loose hair and touch his cheek. "Tell me what happened, Sport."

"The toilet's all clogged up." And then he has another fit, this time smaller and probably crafted for my benefit.

"Is that all?" I say. "Is that the whole problem?" And I give him a wide, carefree smile. I show him the gap in my front teeth, the gap I can shoot a spray of water through. His face relaxes a bit. He's an oversensitive kid—Becky and I know that—and we're trying to equip him with a sense of fun, a joie de vivre. If something breaks, it's broken, no big deal. If a friend calls you a name or throws dirt at you, shake it off. If you can't whistle, hey, you can't whistle. For a month we played that stupid song "Don't Worry, Be Happy," hoping the groove would sink in. But these ploys aren't really working, and anything can set him off. Just the other day a moth fluttered too close to his face—sure, it was a huge hairy moth, I mean, a cousin to Mothra—but he was sobbing like it was the end of the world. It shatters me. The boy's seven years old; he shouldn't be depressed yet.

"Well, Sport," I say, "why don't we hustle on up there and figure this thing out. Okay?"

"Okay," he says.

I lift him off my lap and lower him to the ground as if we're members of some acrobatic family. "Ta-dah," I sing. His socks have left wet blotches all over my pants. "Hey, Sport," I say, pointing to my groin. "Looks like your Dad peed in his pants." He gawks at me oddly, like he doesn't know it's a joke, and then I start to laugh so he'll get to laughing, and finally he does. It's a great laugh, my laugh, open mouthed and joyous—a man's laugh, my father's laugh—and we laugh some more when Josh flaps around like he's wearing soggy clown shoes. Yep, my eyes, my chin, and my laugh; the rest is Becky.

I WAS supposed to take Josh to school, actually just walk with him to the bus stop, but I decided it'd be much more important for him to spend the day with his dad. I had plans. The zoo, a movie, maybe some ice cream, and then back home to cook dinner for Becky—turkey and sweet potatoes with marshmallows on top. It was going to be a good day. But I got tired waking up, I got tired getting out of bed, I got so tired shuffling toward the bathroom that I was too tired to take a shower, and I love taking showers. Becky says it's a stage, a "guy thing." I don't know what the hell that means, but I'm using my vacation days from work because I know if I go there I'll do something stupid like smash a computer or fling sharpened pencils at my secretary; I'd probably call Joe Lester a fucking fat-ass drunk and he'd pull that gun he keeps in his bottom drawer. In the end, no doubt about it, I'd get fired. So now I sit at home in my suit because it makes the boredom seem more productive. "Just wallow," Becky told me before she went to work, "like a duck, quack, quack."

Josh and I walk upstairs. I can see little footprints blurred on the rug; they're the size of my hand. I point to them and say, "You'd make a lousy criminal."

Josh is quiet, solemn, even. As we get closer to the hall

bathroom, he begins to move slower, lingering before each step.

"Ladies and gentlemen of the jury," I say, "the defendant's footprints lead straight to the bathroom." I tousle Josh's hair and then reach down and pull his hand out of his pocket so I can hold it. "It's no big deal, Sport," I say.

He looks up at me. We're in front of the bathroom door. It's closed. Taped to the door is one of his colorful drawings of a military airdrop. Stick-figure paratroopers hang in a flak-filled sky. They're huge, much bigger than the plane they've jumped from, and this lack of perspective seems to have cost them their lives. Death comes with a red crayon.

"I'm not going to be mad," I say to Josh. "I love you." I grab for the doorknob, and I must admit this feeling of suspense settles in my gut. Turds, I'm thinking, are there going to be turds? I imagine them floating near the lip of the toilet bowl, my son's turds, and maybe a few of them have slipped over the side like barrels over Niagara Falls. And this strange thought comes to me: I haven't seen my son's shit in a long time. When he was a baby, then a toddler, Becky and I seemed to be always dealing with it—the diapers, the potty training—but now that he's a middle-aged boy, shit, like so many other things, has snuck into his private world.

"Dad?"

"Yeah?"

Josh makes a gesture with his head, a small tilt—I've seen Becky do the same thing a thousand times—and I realize that I'm just standing there.

"Right," I say.

I open the door. We both pause in the doorway as if we're waiting out an earthquake. There's water on the floor, and it smells dank, like mop water. I look over to the toilet—the shag seat cover is closed—and see no traces of shit on the linoleum. To lighten things up, to take the worry out of Josh's face, I belt out, "I'm singing in the rain, just singing in the rain, what a glorious feeling, I'm happy again," and dance around the bathroom. But Josh seems even more troubled, his wonderful chin lowered into a crescent of soft flesh. "C'mon, Sport," I say, "don't sweat it so much." I go over to the toilet, lift the seat and peer down inside. There are no wads of toilet paper, no floating turds; the water is clear and only slightly higher than average. "This is nothing, Sport," I say. Josh steps into the bathroom. His socks are now gray. "Were you going number two?" I ask.

"Uh . . . no," he says.

"Well, what happened?"

Josh is not a good liar; he's like Becky that way. Their eyes search for an ideal explanation that will somehow forgive the truth. For them lying is like picking a perfect peach. "Nothing," Josh says.

"Then how'd it clog?"

"I'm sorry," he says.

"No, don't worry about it. I'm just curious."

"I don't know."

"Well," I say. And we both stand there. I feel like we're flushing his soon-to-be-dead goldfish down the toilet, saying a few words before Raphael and Leonardo swirl away to the great beyond. "Well," I say again, and I reach over and push down the metal handle.

Josh looks up at me, almost frightened.

"It's a test," I explain.

The water rises with incredible speed. I think of those sub movies when a depth charge hits its mark and men rush for the closing hatch. Josh steps back as the water swells over the side and spreads across the floor. A stray Q-tip floats by. Flotsam or jetsam? I never can remember which is which.

"Oh," Josh says.

"I guess it's still clogged."

He nods.

"Well, Sport," I say, "why don't you hustle downstairs and get us a mop." Josh turns and scoots down the hall. Fresh footprints appear on the rug. I survey the scene, then reach over and grab the plunger from the corner. There is something reassuring about a plunger, something con-stant—that after all these years of technological advance-ment, the plunger has stayed the same, has retained its simple design of slim wooden rod screwed into rubber suc-tion cup. You buy one plunger and it will last you your entire life; it will, in fact, outlast you. Those are things you don't think about in a hardware store.

I hold the plunger over the top-full toilet. There's a dilemma of displacement below me. That's the problem with messy cures, the collateral damage. But I have no choice. I submerge the plunger over the suck hole—I don't know what you call it but it looks like a heel stamped into the porcelain—and start to pump. What with that heel, the churning water sounds like someone running through mud. After six solid thrusts, I stop for a second, then I give it four more. There is no release, no sudden evacuation so satisfy-ing to the domestically incompetent. "Jesus," I say. And then I do something really stupid, I flush the toilet again. The water rises. I slam shut the toilet seat and sit on the shag cozy. Out of sight, out of mind, though my shoes get soaked.

"You tired, Dad?"

I lift my head and glance over at Josh. He doesn't have the mop, but instead has this book that my brother Bruce gave me for my birthday. It's a bizarre book filled with med-ical photographs from late in the last century. When it arrived in the mail Becky shook her head and said, "Typi-cal." Bruce lives in Virginia, and on summer weekends he reenacts Civil War battles. He really fits the part: long beard, bad teeth, and he has the rebel yell down pat. Every Saturday he gets killed in the first wave of the first battle of Bull Run. Poor Josh is very scared of him—I don't blame him—but he loves this book and lugs it around like a talisman. He can spend hours leafing through the pages, studying each picture with utmost concentration, copying a few of them on tracing paper. Sometimes he points one out to me: a Civil War veteran—a young guy, barely in his twenties—coldly displaying the stump of his amputation and the awful infection that resulted. His eyes are so proud and unflinching, I can almost hear him say, *Check out this shit.* And then there are the horrendous photographs of tumors run amok, of dermatolysis, of elephantiasis, of people savaged by their own bodies. I can't believe my Josh looks at this stuff, and I've tried my best to take the book away from him, but he moans like Linus without his blanket. Becky thinks he'll be a doctor, but Jesus, such grim misery can wait.

"Dad?"

"Yeah?"

"You tired, Dad?"

"Tired?"

"Yeah."

"No," I tell him, "I'm fine." Then I say, "Where's the mop?"

Josh breaks down again—I swear his face is made of clay, the way it can crease and sag and fall apart—and while he sobs he tries to talk. He sounds Arabic. "It's all right, Josh." I take him in my arms, his arms still wrapped around that book.

I make out a word. "Leaking," he says.

"What?"

"It's leaking downstairs."

"Leaking?"

He nods.

"Well, okay. Let's investigate." I carry Josh downstairs. "What was it you flushed down the toilet?" I ask him.

"Nothing," and then he adds, "I swear, Daddy."

We walk into the living room and Josh points toward the back wall. A dark stain is on the carpet; on the ceiling a slight seam of water drips every few seconds. "Oops," I say. The two of us watch this slow progress, and standing there, I feel like I'm showing him the moon for the first time. Josh reaches up and touches the ceiling. Water slides down his finger. "We're making a mess," I say. Josh presses his palm against the ceiling. "That's dirty water," I tell him. We go into the kitchen and grab a mop and bucket from the closet.

WHILE I mop the bathroom floor, Josh sits on the sink, the book splayed across his knees, a toothbrush in his mouth even though he's not brushing his teeth.

"Dad," he says.

"Yeah."

"Here." He tilts the book in my direction.

This photograph is one of his favorites, and he's always showing it to me, as if he wants me to read him a story about this bonneted girl, a very normal-looking kid, who wears a lovely dress with an intricate collar and a pinned rose. She could've been going to church, or maybe to an Easter parade, but today she's wants to play. In her raised hands she holds a jump rope. That'll be fun. But something is very wrong with her left foot; it's huge, about six times the size of her other foot. A special boot—the size and color of a prizewinning eggplant—has been crafted by some miracle cobbler. And she stands there, ready to jump rope even though you know there's no way with that foot of hers, and her face, sweet with close-cropped bangs and a timid smile, looks at you with slightly arched eyebrows. It's sad, but it's beyond sad. It's so sad it seems to slip into the hopeful.

"That's something," I say to Josh.

He nods with a certain understanding beyond me. I'd prefer Heidi or Pippi Longstockings.

"A tough break," I say.

Josh leans his head against the medicine-cabinet mirror, and the reflection turns him into a Siamese twin. That'd be a tough way to go through life, especially if you had to share a skull. But today they can separate you, they can fix you, but I wonder if you'd stare at your brother or your sister and try to figure out where you once fit—kneecap to kneecap, spine to spine—if your body was nothing more than a piece of a puzzle.

"Dad?"

"Yeah?"

"The mop."

"Oh. Yeah." I'm holding it like some ridiculous musket, the drenched yarn under my armpit, the yellow handle crossing my chest. "What a space cadet," I say.

"A space cadet?"

"Someone who's out there."

"Out there?"

"Jesus, you're Perry Mason."

"Perry Mason?"

"Oh, never mind." I finish cleaning the floor, wringing out the mop in the bathtub, manipulating the shower to clear away the grime. Everything is finally spotless. "Now the toilet." I clap my hands and rub them together. I ask Josh, "So what's in here?"

"Nothing."

"Really?"

"Yes."

"You sure, Sport?"

"Uh-huh."

"You can tell me, we're buddies."

"Nothing," he says, and I let him get away with lying. I guess it doesn't matter. He seems to be calm at this moment and I don't want to spoil it. I don't want to spoil anything. I pick him up—he splits from the mirror—and tell him to go downstairs and watch TV. "The afternoon is the good time, Sport," I say, "when all the best shows are on. Cartoons galore." He shuffles down the hall. I call out to him, "Not the talk shows, Sport, please no talk shows."

I GRAB the plunger and lift the seat cover, determined to solve this problem for Josh's sake. The toilet looks so ordinary, so benign, but I know there's something lurking in the pipes, and briefly I feel like a hero, like some brave knight confronting a dragon in his home. I stab the plunger through the water and begin the fight. Jab jab jab. But I hear that sound again, the sound of this person running through mud. He's running faster now because something is chasing him, something secret and awful, and this coward is scared. Just keep moving, he thinks, that's all you need to do. He loses one shoe, then another, then he trips and falls but quickly gets up. The mud starts to dry and cake on his skin. It's slowing him down. Keep moving. Please keep moving. Just survive. But his body is starting to give up, convincing his mind to do the same.

I'm sweating all over—I'm in pitiful shape—but my adrenaline has really kicked in. I flush the toilet and plunge through the rising tide, thinking this might help. Faulty reasoning. So much water everywhere. But I keep on going, and after a while I kneel. Blisters are ripening. My back is killing me. Joints ache. At one point I glance over at the doorway and see Josh—I have no idea how long he's been standing there. He watches me, his eyes taking me in as if I'm a picture in his book, some unfortunate soul cast upon the earth. I smile. I must look crazy, the way I'm trying to churn this water into something, anything, but I won't stop until an inkling of hope has surfaced.

Graffiti

It WASN'T A bad job for someone like me, pushing mops and cleaning blackboards. In fact, it was the best job I'd had in a long time. Sometimes I even enjoyed scrubbing the tiny urinals, the tiny desks. It put me in my own little world.

I was sitting at one of those desks, my legs splayed out like wings, talking to Alister, the other janitor. We were on one of our many breaks. Being a night janitor took only two hours of real work; the rest of the time was spent smoking or drinking or shooting hoops at the gym with the security guard.

"I made my bathroom light go off," Alister was telling me. "I was in bed and I didn't want to get up so I just shot my brain at the switch and it clicked off." He snapped his fingers. "Like that." Alister had been a janitor at St. Vincent's Elementary for twelve years and was too accustomed to ammonium chloride. His eyes were glass buttons and the corners of his mouth collected an odd milky substance. He straightened up in his chair and said, "Here, watch," and after a few seconds of flexing his facial muscles, he stared hard at the discarded bucket and mop in the middle of the classroom. His palms went to his temples, his eyes strained. This lasted a minute. "There," he said, his face loosening. "Did you see that?"

"What?"

"The handle—it twitched." Alister had fantasies about letting his mind do all the work, like Mickey Mouse in *The Sorcerer's Apprentice*. "Someday, Dave, it'll happen. This place'll be plugged into my brain."

ONCE in a while, during the day, I'd pretend that I had left something behind in the custodial closet and I'd come back to the school and walk the halls of the first and second and third graders. The teachers were mostly women. They were beautiful and all seemed recently married, a few years away from having kids themselves. The girls and boys must have loved them—the Mrs. Andrews, the Mrs. Kirklands. I'd eavesdrop on basic math, on beginning English, on weather patterns and why it rains, and during storytelling I'd bend down and pretend to tie my shoes for a good five minutes. Those soft voices, the gentle pronunciations. But most of the time I tried to make my visit coincide with recess or lunch. The children would be hopping down the halls and they would brush against my sides. I'd lift up my arms, carried on a stream of pigtails and bowl cuts.

VINCE, the security guard, came around quite often, walking with an apple stuck in his mouth, intrigued by the power of his own teeth, especially the ability to grip and scar. Vince had visions of State Patrol, of those crisp hats and sleek nine millimeters. He enjoyed talking to me, because for a short time I had been in prison.

"Now, how did it work?" he asked.

"What?" I was erasing a blackboard with a damp cloth.

"The scam."

"It was no big deal," I told him, making my way along the blackboard, the words disappearing under each sweep of my hand. The newly wet slate resembled a windshield at night with a long expanse of empty road stretching out in front of it. Then it fogged dry.

"C'mon, just tell me again." Vince sat down at the teacher's desk.

"It was called 'End Hunger Now.' "

"They were going to save Cambodia," Alister said, moving his mop in a lazy arc.

"No, Ethiopia."

"Right, Africa." Alister bent down to the lip of the yellow bucket and listened as if it were the opening of a mysterious shell. He said a hollow "Charity."

Vince had a smile on his face. "And it was all phony."

I nodded.

"How much did you take in before Johnny Fuzz?"

"About fifty thousand. But I was just the footman. I answered phones, took credit-card numbers. That's it. For a while I even thought I was doing some good, that there were actually victims out there."

"Shit," Vince said. "And they sent you to the pen for that?"

"I also had a couple of bad checks floating around."

"Hello," Alister said into the bucket.

"But the Big House?" asked Vince.

Books and TV, I thought, that's what prison is, with incredible flashes of violence thrown in between. I made my way to the erasers.

Alister grabbed the mop and dumped its gray yarn into the bucket as if he were drowning a dog.

THE NEXT afternoon I walked by the community center three or four times before I went in. The building was an old bomb shelter, the outside walls two feet thick and windowless and painted pink in absurd hope of making it appear dainty, like a giant box of Kleenex. I had always pictured the inside to be a place where children cut out construction-paper flowers and stuck them to the walls; where old people talked of the old days and collected raffle tickets for some upcoming dance. But instead it was all white light and metal furniture and a curtain, a ratty red velvet, which hid something away—rations of canned food? gas masks? Of the three desks, only one was occupied, and the occupant seemed as if she had been trapped inside this bunker since a war known only to herself. I asked her about the possibilities of volunteering, of helping others in need, and she pointed toward the corner and said, "Try the Good Samaritan Board."

I glanced in the direction of her finger. "Okay, thanks."

The Good Samaritan Board was covered with tacked-up yellow, blue, and white note cards. It was a mosaic of pain. A paraplegic needs someone to rub his useless legs. A stroke victim needs someone to give her twice-weekly drives to the physical therapist. A terminal-cancer case needs someone to adopt her dog. I stood there, hands in pockets, reading up and down, taking in every word underlined and punched with exclamation. *Please! Thank You!* All these wrecked bodies waiting at home for a savior, and all I had to do was reach out and pick one. But there were too many choices. It was like being at a video store with all those movies and trying to find the perfect one that would salvage your Saturday night.

I closed my eyes and grabbed a card at random and carried it outside with me, like a ticket of admission. Written in a textbook cursive, the letters were round and well connected: A blind woman needs someone to read to her. By the time I was halfway down Main Street, and standing in front of Red's Saloon, draft beers for a buck, I had the phone number memorized. The digits added up to forty-one, which has nothing to do with anything but is something I always do with phone numbers.

THE patrons of Red's were hunched over the bar as if stationed on an assembly line picking out the bad peanuts from the good. On the raised TV a nature program played. A tortoise, long past struggling, was dying on its back. An English voice narrated and made things sound beautiful.

I went over to the phone. On the third ring, someone answered.

"Hello?"

"Yes, hi, is this Mrs. Freninger?"

"Did I win a prize or something?"

"Well, no."

"Didn't think so. So what do you want?"

"Well, Mrs. Freninger, I'm calling about your—"

"Car? I sold it. The kid screwed me, too."

"No, no, I'm calling about your notice for someone to read to you."

"Jesus, I put that up ages ago."

"Well, I'm looking to do some volunteer work."

"Are you a misdemeanor or a student?"

"Neither, really. I just want to do something decent."

"Ha. Help the little old blind lady, huh?"

"Well—"

"What movie star do you look like?"

"What?"

"C'mon, I'm not going to touch your face, I find that whole concept disgusting and uninformative."

"I guess a skinny, shorter, non-ethnic Victor Mature." *The Robe* was my favorite movie as a kid. But I probably look more like Joey Bishop.

"He was an awful actor. Well, Victor, can you read clearly?"

"Sure."

"Did you go to college?"

"Yeah." I spent a year at the community college.

"What do you do for a living?"

"I'm a carpenter." My mind was still on *The Robe,* and I figured everyone trusts a carpenter. No one trusts a night janitor. Or Joey Bishop.

"Well, Victor—"

"It's Dave."

"I don't know Dave, I know Victor Mature. Why don't you come over at six o'clock on Thursday. We'll have a trial read." Then she gave me her address. She didn't live too far away. Before hanging up she told me she had a dog. "A German shepherd," she said with an edge of threat.

AT WORK, Alister sat at a third-grader's desk. In his hand he held a Mr. Clean–soaked rag, which he occasionally brought to his nose. "Yesterday," he said, "I changed the channels with my head. Flick, *Oprah*. Flick, QVC. Flick, CNN. Flick, Stovetop Stuffing. My mind on remote control."

I was wiping down the blackboard's last lesson. *The boy was sad. The boy is now happy. The boy will be sad again.* "A bit depressing," I said.

"No, I was doing it. I've got power." He started to scrub the desk. *"Mr. Vickers is a fag."*

"What?"

He pointed to the desktop. "Says it right here: *Mr. Vickers is a fag.*" Alister laughed. *"Mr. Vickers sucks cock."*

I walked over to Alister.

"Mr. Vickers eats kids' crap. Jesus, these kids are something."

"Nailed the plural possessive," I said.

"Poor Mr. Vickers."

"A good teacher, though."

Alister breathed on the desk and rubbed the writing away. Mr. Vickers was easily restored.

MRS. Freninger's house was a nice house, a house that belonged in a row of houses. Alone, it would be ridiculous, but here, with the other houses on this street, it fulfilled a moving picture of community.

I was smoking, watching the windows, but there wasn't

much to see. Gauzy curtains blurred the inside. I had a feeling of stage fright. Disabilities and deformities make me anxious. I try to act naturally by striking some nonchalant pose between noticing and not noticing, but in the end I'm not a good enough actor. I finished the cigarette and flicked it on her well-kept lawn, knowing that litter would be overlooked. After climbing the steps and opening the screen door, I paused before knocking. It felt like a date, a first date.

Mrs. Freninger was quick to answer. "Yes?"

She was taller than I thought a blind woman should be, and firmer, but I was glad that she wore dark glasses, though the frames seemed too stylish. I feared dead milky eyes—or worse, empty sockets. The only other thing I gathered, besides her sharp nose, well-defined chin, and pulled-back blond-gray hair, was that she wore a healthy application of Tulsa-red lipstick.

"Hello, Mrs. Freninger."

"Is this Victor?"

"Yes."

"You smoke, Victor?"

"Yes."

"You drink?"

"Well . . ."

"I hate the smell of smoke and drink. And I hate cologne, especially Brut and Canoe."

"I don't wear cologne."

"I know."

She angled her head as if hearing my features in the shape of my plain words. "Well, come in and sit down in the far-right chair, it has the best light." She moved aside so that I could pass, then she went to the couch, maneuvering around a coffee table and a sleeping dog. Everything in the room was clean and tidy except for dust on the lamp shades. Books were arranged in three bookshelves.

I squirmed in my chair. "Nice place," I said.

"How old are you?"

"Thirty-one. Nice dog." I clicked my tongue, but the dog didn't move.

"Some society gave him to me. But I'm sorry, I'm not going to let a stupid dog lead me around. Too degrading. And canes are out of the question. Tap, tap, tap. I don't think so."

My left knee rocked up and down, a nervous habit. "Well . . ."

"A year ago, Victor. Went to get my lashes dyed but the beautician screwed up and sprayed the junk in my eyes. I sued and lost. My husband's gone and run off to California to pursue some absurd acting career. I don't watch TV because sometimes his sly voice comes on telling me to buy a Buick or a Friendly's shake. I've lived in this town all my life and no one likes me much, which is fine. A hired friend comes over three times a week. She's Mexican."

"Well . . ."

"I just wanted to let you know my sad tale, Victor. Now yours."

"What?"

"C'mon, spill it."

I leaned forward and lifted one hand high in the air, then another; I proceeded to wave them wildly as if on a roller-coaster. "I moved into town recently. I'm a carpenter, a free-lance carpenter." Was there such a thing? I had no idea. "I've been to college," I said, pretending to swim, cupped hand stroking after cupped hand. "I wanted to be a doctor but was no good in science." I pinched my nose and drowned. "I grew up in Hartford." I've never been to Hartford, but I added, for authenticity, "I hated that dump." During this whole performance her face remained unchanged.

"Fascinating, Victor." She crossed her long legs. She wore black stockings that tapered into high heels. "On the table by your left hand is a book. Pick it up."

It was *Adam Bede,* by George Eliot. I knew *Middle-march*—Dorothea Brooke and Lydgate and all the rest; I had read it in jail, like so many other soft-timers. It helped you get an early parole. The warden believed that literature could rehabilitate the nonviolent offender, and he especially appreciated Eliot's sense of justice. But this book I didn't know.

"I love George Eliot," Mrs. Freninger said. "So detailed, everything placed before you. But I haven't read *Adam Bede.* I always hated the title." She sat back, her arms stretching along the slope of the couch. I stuck my tongue out at her. I picked my nose. I put on a silly face. "Please, read," she said.

The spine of the old book cracked, and the pages left dusty traces on my fingers. I coughed a few times, then swallowed and rested my feet on the coffee table. *"Book One, Chapter I, The Workshop."* I paused for effect. *"With a single drop of ink for a mirror, the Egyptian sorcerer undertakes to reveal to any chance comer far-reaching visions of the past. This is what I undertake to do for you, reader. With this drop of ink at the end of my pen, I will show you the roomy workshop of Mr. Jonathan Burge, carpenter and builder, in the village of Hayslope, as it appeared on the eighteenth of June, in the year of our Lord 1799."* I stopped and looked to her for approval. I had read flawlessly.

"Sounds like you and Mr. Burge have something in common," she said.

"What?"

"Both carpenters."

"Oh yeah, right."

She sat back. "Continue, please, and a little slower," she said. "Punctuate."

I read for over an hour, with my throat becoming increasingly dry and sore. Halfway through, as the sun lowered, lights clicked on all over the house. "They're on a timer," Mrs. Freninger said. And after I finished the fourth chapter,

"Home and Its Sorrows," I closed the book. It was time for work. "Well, thank you, Victor." She seemed pensive, a bit tired. Light reflected from her glasses. I flapped my arms in a bad impersonation of a chicken, then I grabbed my crotch, but her face didn't change, and the dog by her side hadn't moved since my arrival. As I was leaving, Mrs. Freninger asked me to come close to her. She lifted up a small tape recorder. "Give me your phone number, Victor."

ALISTER, Vince and I shot hoops in the school gym that night. We played Horse. Alister couldn't sink a thing and was out almost instantly, but he didn't care. Vince and I were even at H-O.

"So what's this blind lady like?" Vince asked.

"All right." I missed. H-O-R.

"Are her eyes all fucked up?" Before Vince shot, he bounced the ball against his head a few times. This annoyed me.

"No, she's attractive." I missed again. H-O-R-S. "Kind of like Barbara Stanwyck—an older Barbara Stanwyck, like when she was in *The Big Valley*."

"Huh?"

"You know, that *Bonanza* ripoff, with Lee Majors and Linda Evans."

"Ah, shit, too bad she's doesn't look like Linda Evans." Vince picked at his undershirt. "Then we could go over there and do all sorts of nasty stuff. How'd she know who it was? The perfect crime." Vince winked at me, then shot and missed. H-O-R. "Dammit." He retrieved the ball and slapped at it as if he were slapping a face. Then he passed it to me.

I missed.

Vince made an opposite hand layup, something I'm lousy at, and he won. "I'll tell you what," he said. "I'll give you an exclamation point."

"That's all right, I'm done."

"C'mon, let's keep it going. How about a quick game of Pig?"

"Nope."

We had to help Alister to his feet; he'd been feeling dizzy. "Thanks, guys," he said. "For a second there I thought you were throwing my head around."

"THE mirror is doubtless defective. The outlines will sometimes be disturbed, the reflection faint or confused; but I feel as much bound to tell you as precisely as I can what that reflection is, as if I were in the witness-box, narrating my experience on oath."

"Excuse me, Victor." Mrs. Freninger rose from the couch and straightened her skirt. "I hate to stop you, but I need to pee." She left down the hall, each step confident. I heard a door shut.

I got up, moved a lamp, moved a side table, moved her glass of water to the farthest edge of the coffee table, moved a throw pillow, moved a porcelain figurine, an elephant, to the middle of the room, moved the hour hand of the grandfather clock back two hours, moved the couch six inches, moved a wastepaper basket. When Mrs. Freninger returned, she still maneuvered with precision, still plopped down onto the couch, still found her glass of water. "Victor," she said.

"Yes."

"Have you been drinking?"

"Yes."

"Well, you stink. And your reading's a bit sloppy. Continue." When I came back a few days later, the house had been returned to its original state. But Mrs. Freninger didn't say a word, gave no hint of knowing anything.

I HAD started drinking during the day, at first in my apartment, then out at Red's. I met a woman there. She was paying for her drinks in change pulled out of a sock. "I was going to do my laundry," she said. "But fuck it." I smiled. I was smiling at everything. "*You* certainly could use a wash," she told me, and she reached over and grabbed me by the belt. Her name was Kat. The other people at the bar looked over, shaking their heads while Kat and I hit it off. She giggled and leaned into the curve of my neck. "You're funny," she said. I don't remember making any jokes, but I went with it. We left together. Back at my apartment, our clothes off, she guided her tits into my mouth; they tasted of bleach. She wanted me to grab at the Saturn tattoo on her inner thigh. "Pinch it," she said. And she wanted me to suck the Jupiter tattoo just above her collarbone. "That's right, suck it," she said. I felt as if I were hurling through space, untethered to the mother ship, my oxygen running out. "Bite Neptune," she ordered, but I couldn't spot the little blue planet eighth from the sun. "C'mon, bite it," she said. And I found myself having momentary visions of my past. They came in little flashes, but they didn't make any sense to me. It was like watching a stranger's slide show. "C'mon." She slapped me on the side of the head.

SOON, I began to change the story, at first bit by bit. Adam Bede loosens up, enjoying a laugh in the middle of stern pronouncements. "*It smells very sweet,*" *he said;* "*those stripped uns have no smell. Stick it up your frock and it will smell a plenty, and then you can put it in water after.*" Mrs. Freninger didn't seem to notice. After a while, I made up whole paragraphs, introduced new characters, and, in general, caused chaos in the tiny village of Hayslope. Only once did she ever question anything.

"Victor."

"Yes," I said.

"Is there really a character named Dinah Shore?"

"Yes."

"I hated Dinah Shore, the singer Dinah Shore, not the young Methodist preacher. She I like. But the singer, too sunny."

IT WAS on a Tuesday that I decided to stop showering for a while. And I didn't brush my teeth anymore. I also began to eat meals heavy with garlic and onions and rarely changed my clothes. The odor that came from me was strong, like wet leaves burning.

"Jesus, you're ripe," Mrs. Freninger said at the door. "Can't you take a shower before coming here?"

"Sorry, I had to finish building a porch." I walked over to the chair and plugged in a tape player.

"What are you doing?" she asked.

"Just getting ready." I sat down.

She moved toward the couch but paused in the middle of the room, her chin slightly raised, the same way Grace Kelly raised her chin to Jimmy Stewart. "Do you want anything to drink?" she asked.

"No, I'm fine."

"Some water?"

"No, thanks."

She took her seat. "Okay," she said. "I'm ready."

I pushed down the "play" button. The cheap tape player's internal mechanism began to whirr. My voice emerged from the tiny speaker; distant and breathless and secretive, as recorded that morning in bed. "*Book Five. Chapter XXXVI. The Journey in Hope. A long, lonely journey, with sadness in the heart; away from the familiar to the strange: that is a hard and dreary thing even to the rich, the strong, the instructed; a hard thing, even when we are called by duty, not urged by dread.*" I watched her face closely. She must have recognized the difference—it was obvious—but she didn't let on.

"A little louder, please," she said.

I reached over and turned up the volume. My voice rose. "Thank you," she said.

A pair of binoculars hung around my neck, and I lifted them, focusing on Mrs. Freninger's face. I had to squint to smooth the blurs. It was amazing to watch her so closely. She was in the adolescence of late middle age, where beauty turns sluggish on its way to the shady side—or so George Eliot might have written. Faded freckles gave away an old love for the sun. Her hair was trapped in a bun. And a mysterious scar, about a half-inch long, slanted into those heavily made-up lips, so thin a scalpel seemed the only possible cause. On my lap was a leather photo album pilfered from one of the bookcase shelves. The snapshots inside showed a younger Mrs. Freninger, reluctant to smile, as if she knew that such a display was too easy. She was a woman quite used to the fact that people liked to look at her, and this allowed her a certain seriousness. Those eyes staring at you, even then, held a coldness as if they had glimpsed their eventual fate in dim, ill-defined pictures. I tried to see her as the reckless Hetty, the love of Adam Bede's life, churning the butter on Hall Farm and dreaming of Arthur Donnithorne, that dashing squire.

"Victor."

I reached over and pushed down the "stop" button. It made a plastic click.

"Yes."

"Oh, nothing." She waved her left hand. "Go ahead."

I restarted the tape and continued to watch her reactions through the binoculars. I thought I caught a hairy arch of an eyebrow above her dark glasses when Hetty met a poacher in the private game preserve called the Chase. He was smoking a cigarette by a tree, a brace of pheasant at his feet, a can of beer in his hand.

" 'Hey there,' the poacher said.

" 'Hi,' Hetty answered. *She was not unaccustomed to sur-*

prises, in fact she quite enjoyed them. 'Who are you?' she asked.

" 'Your local poacher.'

"Hetty stepped back, briefly afraid of such a man. The epithet, 'A thief,' regretfully slipped from her well-formed lips.

"The poacher smiled without joy. 'Our deeds determine us, as much as we determine our deeds, and until we know what has been or will be the peculiar combination of outward with inward facts, which constitutes a man's actions, it will be better not to think ourselves wise to his character.' He stubbed his cigarette against his clodhoppers. 'I read that somewhere,' he said.

" 'Oh' was Hetty's reply. 'Oh,' she said again, and then she was offered a beer."

We both listened with growing curiosity.

And at the end of the chapter Mrs. Freninger asked me for a cigarette. "I used to smoke," she said.

I lit two cigarettes, borrowing Paul Henreid's technique in *Now, Voyager.* I placed one of them in the waiting V of her fingers. She brought it to her lips and inhaled, then exhaled expertly through her nostrils. The smoke seemed suited to her, reluctant to dissipate. "I quit years ago," she told me. "And all my ashtrays became decorative."

"Uh-huh."

After every few drags, I guided her hand to the ashtray, tapping off the ash for her. Lipstick stained the filter. "It was once glamorous, Victor. Now it's disgusting and offensive. Maybe I'll take it up again."

"Why not," I figured.

"A bit of a head rush," she said. "Like I'm a teenager again."

We smoked until the feet of the Camel emblem burned. Then I left.

• • •

WHILE cleaning the classroom one night, Alister fell to the floor and started to roll as if on fire. He shouted at things I couldn't see. I dropped on top of him and restrained him. He battled me all the way. "I'll bend you across this classroom." "Bend" was his new word.

"Just calm down," I whispered in his ear. Foam started to spill from his mouth. I didn't think humans actually did that. I tried wiping the stuff away—it was warm on my hand— but he seemed to have an endless supply. "Just calm down," I said over and over again.

"I can bend it all, Dave," he shouted. A beard of froth hung from his chin; he was a crazed Rip Van Winkle struggling against his sleep.

"Of course you can." I began yelling for help, hoping Vince would hear.

A light flickered. "I did that," Alister told me.

"Sure," I said.

And later, before the ambulance arrived, a bird flew into one of the windows. "I did that," he told me again.

AT OUR next reading, with the tape player on, I began to write notes to Mrs. Freninger along the baseboards, in the corners, on sills. *Please recycle. Free Tibet. Down with meat.* I wrote my words in a crimped hand, the letters blocked and unidentifiable. I'd walk around the room and choose a particular spot. "I hope you don't mind me moving, I need to stretch my legs."

"No, not at all."

I used a felt-tip pen. *UNICEF. March of Dimes. Save the Children.* From a distance the phrases looked like resting centipedes. And sometimes they seemed to scurry. While I wrote, I heard myself describing poor Hetty's murder trial. No matter how much I tried to change the story, Hetty still ended up killing her illegitimate newborn in a fit of hopeless despair. And now she was doomed to the consequences of her vanity and lust. Only her prison-cell confession could salvage her soul.

"*Hetty was silent, but she shuddered again, as if there was still something behind; and Dinah waited, for her heart was so full that tears must come before words. At last, Hetty burst out, with a sob,*

" '*Dinah, do you think God will take away that crying and the place in the wood, now I've told everything?'*

" '*Let us pray, poor sinner. Let us fall on our knees again, and pray to the God of all mercy.' *"

I stopped the tape and said, "End of Chapter X-L-V," pronouncing the Roman numerals, as if describing the size of the tragedy.

"Pretty heavy." Mrs. Freninger stretched her neck left, then right, her muscles stiffened by listening. "Of course that lech Arthur Donnithorne gets off scot-free while beautiful Hetty has to hang. Typical." She leaned forward, her hands crossed over each other and her dark glasses fixed on me. "Hey, Victor."

"Yeah."

"When does that poacher return?"

I unplugged the tape player, wrapping the cord in a lasso. "I'm not sure."

"I liked him," she said.

"Don't know, I haven't finished the book either." I got up from the chair.

"How much longer do we have?"

"After 'The Hours of Suspense,' seventy more pages."

"The end is near."

"Yes," I said.

FOR THE next two weeks, I avoided Mrs. Freninger, not showing up at the usual time in the afternoon. I wasn't in the mood to go on, preferring Hetty trapped in jail, the gallows still pages away, the exact conclusions of that world unknown to the two of us. During the day I treated my apartment as a cell, not leaving, just watching soap operas. It didn't take long to reacquaint myself with the plots. And the talk shows were all the same. Everything passed as intrigue, and deceptions sold products. "Money-back guarantee!" "First month free!" "Zero down!" The announcers shouted at me, their voices perfect for the pitch. "It's just that easy!" At night I worked with a new guy at the school, Stan, a humorless sort who made comments about second-hand smoke and poor health coverage. His only delusion was that he thought this job was temporary. I missed the fuller delusions of Alister.

Then Mrs. Freninger started to call. "Victor, where the hell have you been?"

"Sorry, I've been busy."

"That's no excuse," she said. "We're close to the end."

"I haven't had time."

"Victor."

"I'll be by Thursday."

And when I missed that meeting she called again, her voice a little more anxious. "Victor, get over here," she said. I pictured her kicking the dog in frustration.

"Tomorrow," I said.

"You better be here."

"Tomorrow."

But I wanted her to wait. And over the next few days, when the phone rang, I didn't bother to pick it up, knowing that when something is finished, the next step is to forget it unless you can turn it into something else.

THERE is a moment in *Adam Bede*, toward the end, which I now read over and over again. It's about love's gradual approach: *Those slight words and looks and touches are part of the soul's language; and the finest language, I believe, is chiefly made up of unimposing words, such as "light," "sound," "stars," "music"—words really not worth looking at, or hearing, in themselves, any more than "chips" or "sawdust." It is only that they happen to be the signs of something unspeakably great and beautiful. I am of the opinion that love is a great thing and beautiful thing too, and if you agree with me, the smallest signs of it will not be chips and sawdust to you; they will rather be like those little words "light" and "music," stirring the long-winding fibres of your memory and enriching your present with your most precious past.*

ON MONDAY, I left work early, in the middle of cleaning a classroom, and Stan overreacted. He said it was bullshit, he even used the term "unprofessional," but I just waved him away. When I burst through the metal doors—still, after all these years of not being in school, an exciting moment of release—there was nothing outside. It was two in the morning. I don't know what I was expecting, some sound track swelling to crescendo, a group of cheering friends, but there was nothing except a mist not yet fallen into dew. And as I stood within that close air, I began to sense I was a boy again and I was sick in bed and my mother had set up a humidifier in the corner of my room so that I might be able to breathe.

Mrs. Freninger didn't live far away. The windows of her house were dark, as were all the other windows on that perfect street. I sat on the steps and smoked. I flicked the cigarette on the lawn, got up, and rang the bell for a full minute until she opened the front door.

"Hello?"

"It's me," I said.

"Victor?" Her chin bumped against the screen. She wasn't wearing those useless glasses, and this seemed to make her more blind.

"I hope I didn't wake you."

"Well, actually, no. I was awake. I'm a bit of an insomniac." She opened the door and moved aside to let me in. "Everything okay?"

I went from lamp to lamp and turned each on, her head following me with every click. I narrated my actions for her. "I'm turning on the lights." I took off the lamp shades and piled them in the corner. "I'm removing the lamp shades." The room was now bright and merciless. She was wearing a silk bathrobe the color of a peach. Her toenails were painted red. And I saw her eyes for the first time. I stepped closer. They were completely black, as if each pupil had been poked with something sharp and the ink had bled into the iris and then run into the rest of the eye. "I thought we might finish *Adam Bede*," I said.

"Right now?"

"Yes."

She nodded before answering, "All right," then walked to the couch and sat down. Her combed-out hair hung to her shoulders. "Hetty's on her way to her execution," she said.

"Yes. 'The Hours of Suspense.' "

"That's right."

I began to take off my clothes. She heard me undo my belt, heel off my sneakers. "What are you doing?" she asked.

"The flesh is weak, as Dinah Shore might say."

Mrs. Freninger smiled and then wiped at her mouth as if something had grazed her lips. She pulled her legs up into her chest and held her feet in her hands. She rested her chin on her knees. "Is this part of the ending?" she asked.

"No story is the same to us after a lapse of time; or rather, we who read it are no longer the same interpreters," I said, cribbing from the text. In that harsh light, Mrs. Freninger watched my voice, her black eyes reflecting my pitiful body, the reflection faint or confused but definitely there.

Naked now, in the middle of the room, I held *Adam Bede* in one hand, a Magic Marker in the other. There are words that you use to describe impossible things, though these words do no justice to your memory of the event. But still, you try.

I started on the left side of the room, and as the pen flowed in large and small loops over the wall, I told her my story. Soon, my pen would touch her.

Opening Day

I T WAS THE Spring I tried to Save My Marriage, the Spring I made an effort to be My Old Self again. On weekends I visited the house and devised basic repairs from the effects of winter. I replaced storm windows with screen windows, cutting up my fingers in the process. I fertilized and mulched the quarter acre of stubborn land. I made sure the tree house was still solid after the record snows and put in a few nails for good measure. And finally I built a fence, a white picket job, that edged the perimeter of the property like a set of movie-star teeth. After this, my wife invited me over for a Family Dinner.

"Roast beef," she told me on the phone.

"Well, sure," I said. "That'd be great." My thumb was nervous on the remote's mute button, as if she could somehow hear me waste time. My new shame was TV, and whenever I was in that small apartment, the TV was on. I especially liked C-Span's coverage of the British House of Commons, everyone shouting and murmuring with basic good humor, often instructing their Right Honorable Friends to shove it up their asses.

"How about Friday?" she said.

"Friday's fine."

"Good." And then there was an awkward silence

between the two of us, a moment of indecision. Instead of the usual End of Conversation abruptness, we had time to wait for the other to hang up. It seemed to baffle us.

THIS WAS also the Spring the Cleveland Indians were touted as American League contenders. Losers for as long as anyone cared to remember, Cellar Dwellers season after season, the team finally had a chance at greatness. I was a fan. In elementary school, I felt physically ill with each defeat; in junior high and high school, I switched allegiance to the Cincinnati Reds; and in three semesters before flunking out of Ohio State, I rekindled my loyalty and started to take a certain pride in the losing traditions of the ball club. During home games I'd sit in the stands of that old Municipal Stadium, and I'd drink beer after beer in those waxy cups, the bottoms sagging against my thigh, until late in the innings, when I'd sneak up into the empty Nose Bleeds and stretch out on the bleachers. The noise of distant incompetence lulled me into a comfortable sleep. Sometimes, My Old Man came along, and he'd shout at the players to "C'mon, Hustle Up!" and "Give It Your All!" his voice filled with an awkward desperation. And I remember once turning to look at him after the Indians had blown a lead, a smug smile already on my face, and seeing him pinch himself on the arm, hard enough to leave a three-day bruise.

"They Break Your Heart," he said.

"You take it too seriously."

"Just shut up."

But this Spring promised to be different. The Tribe was stocked with a bunch of solid players, and they had a prized new Tepee—Jacob's Field—designed to bring back memories of The Good Old Days. Eccentric angles, intimate surroundings, the stadium was considered the third step in the Revitalization of Cleveland. Number four was the Rock and Roll Hall of Fame. Gazing toward the future, the Chamber of Commerce tried to wipe out the last thirty years with a thermonuclear blast of development. My days, it was generally accepted, were days to forget.

THAT Friday night I took a taxi to my house, passing through Rockefeller Park on my way to Richmond Heights. Garfield's Tomb was just starting to attract its usual crowd of Misdemeanors. They lingered like a whisper to the past. "Some kind of dance or something tonight?" the cabbie asked, his eyes catching me in the rear-view mirror.

"No. Having dinner at home."

"Good for You," he said. This guy often drove me around during The Year My License Was Suspended; he didn't turn on the meter until halfway there. "You guys might get back together, you think?"

"Who knows?"

"But that's good."

"We'll see."

The cars on Euclid Ave. were filled with kids, this being The Strip. Elaborate horns and funky lights battled for attention, no one able to afford a real souped-up rig. At stoplights the shouting began, mostly taunts to Eat My Shit, You Candyass Motherfucker, or sometimes a question of Where You Going Tonight? If these kids weren't drunk or high, they were doing a pretty good job of acting that way. I watched from the stuck-open window, my hands on my lap as if they were handcuffed.

When the light changed and the cars began to move again, a breeze rushed in. I slid to the middle to avoid mussing up my hair.

"So to your house then, not the Mall?" he asked me.

"No, the Mall. I'll walk after that."

"Whatever suits you fine."

THE Richmond Mall was like an airport without airplanes, and the people inside wandered around killing time, waiting for some unfortunate delay to end. A large wishing fountain drizzled in the main terminal, though nobody threw in any change, and fake plants struggled in an environment where seasons were defined by the "Sale" signs in storefront windows. Elderly couples sat on benches and watched the circling adolescents. Sober entertainments were advertised with blinking lights, the video arcade posting a small notice that warned epileptics of The Possible Danger Of Some Games. I wondered which ones to avoid. I also wondered if you could still buy drugs in the bathroom.

I went into Norman's Sporting Goods—the air almost lonely without the smell of sweat—and walked toward the baseball section. A full uniform hung from the pegboard wall, like an invisible Christ crucified for poor pitching. Below, aluminum and ash bats leaned in a line, their weight marked on the heel. I picked up a Louisiana Slugger and took a few lazy swings. It felt nice and simple, this back-and-forth movement, though my playing days had been Nothing to Write Home About.

Another display carried a slew of baseball mitts, each waiting for a hand to slip in. I grabbed a Raleigh with Barry Bonds's autograph across the thumb and pounded the leather with my free fist. I crouched down in the ready position; I scooped up an imaginary grounder; I threw to first. An Easy Out. That was my type of hit, worthless without an error.

A young man came over and said, "May I Help You?" He held an accordion of New York Yankee hats.

"Is this mitt any good?" I asked.

"Sure, once you break it in."

"Okay. And I need another, for a six-year-old boy. A lefty."

The young man pointed an elbow toward the bottom of the rack. "Go low," he said. "Lefties have an 'L' sticker in the palm."

I slid one free. "Is this the right size?"

"I really couldn't tell you," he said.

• • •

WITH the Norman's Sporting Goods bag bumping against my leg, I made my way down an alley, dodging potholes filled with water. This was a shortcut. From here, you could see the back porches of the neighborhood, the kitchen windows steamed with cooking food. Blue recycling bins were stacked next to the doors, and a few people had compost piles in their yards. Though I had been away only a year, this was new to me. All that sorting and arranging would've driven me nuts, judging between the garbage to be reborn and the garbage to be damned, as if Dixie Cups had a soul.

I loitered around, killing time, waiting for 7:30 P.M. on the dot. Lateness was once The Least of My Problems.

"Hey, that you?" a familiar voice called out.

I slid off the hood of a parked car, almost half a block from the house. "How do you see me?" I asked.

"I don't. Just figured you'd be lurking around." She stood in the doorway, the screen door leaning against her body. The streetlight cast light on her face, and seeing that smile again, both forgiving and condemning, almost made me take off in the opposite direction. But I picked up my bag and started forward.

"You been waiting long?"

"Not really."

She kissed me on the cheek, her hand intimate on my neck. I hated that I noticed her makeup, her perfume, her hairdo—hell, I should've been pleased—but it seemed like she was making too much of an effort For Things to Work Out. Then again, I had shaved that afternoon and remembered to hold off on the aftershave. She never trusted that smell, always thinking there was a taint hidden underneath.

"What's in the bag?"

"Some stuff. Belated presents, I guess."

"Oh, great." She led me into the kitchen. The linoleum on the floor was peeling at the corners, no doubt another problem to repair. She went over and peeked into the oven, sizzles emerging from the darkness. "Take a look," she said.

I glanced over her shoulder. "Yum."

"Be ready in twenty minutes. Hope You're Hungry." She checked the pots on the electric coils—peas and mashed potatoes and gravy—and checked the bread in the toaster. She played the oven like a church organ. "Hot in here, isn't it?" she said, the back of her hand dabbing her chin.

I wiped my forehead and said Yes.

IN THE living room, sitting properly on the couch, my son watched the TV even though it wasn't on. I wondered if he caught his reflection in the curved gray glass and pretended that his life was part of a ridiculous show.

"What's on?" I asked.

"Mom doesn't let me watch with company."

"Is there often company?"

"Sure."

I sat on the arm of the couch and tried to be The Casual Father Just Home From Work. But my son wasn't interested in me. With both hands he held a glass of Coke firmly on his lap. He seemed to be wearing his Sunday Best without the jacket and tie, his ears straining for a Sermon.

"You can't do that," he suddenly told me.

"What?" I was ready for an outpouring of six-year-old bitterness: Mr. Rogers meets Oprah.

"Sit on the couch like that. Mom doesn't let that."

"Oh. Got it." I sprung up and bounced on my toes, as if the slipcover had suddenly turned red-hot, then I paced around, inspecting the bric-a-brac on the shelves. A collection of figurine pigs had been started while I was away. After my brief lap, I came back to the couch.

"You have pennies in those loafers?" I asked.

"I got quarters in case I need to make a call. Like I got quarters in my socks when I'm wearing sneaks."

"Smart."

He nodded the way kids do—all chin.

"Who do you call when there's trouble?"

"Mom, unless Mom's in trouble. Then it's nine-one-one and the cops come."

"That's very good."

A silence slipped in, and we both stared at the blank TV and waited for something to happen.

SHE came in with two glasses of very sweet iced tea, her face all blatant joy with the vision of Her Two Men together. "I thought you guys had left, so quiet in here." She handed me a glass. "This'll cool you down."

I thanked her.

"Dinner will be ready soon. But let's see what you brought us." She took a seat next to the boy, her hands re-arranging her skirt. Her present was an afterthought to the baseball gloves, just a gesture from the Hallmark store, but I could tell from her giddy anticipation that she expected more. And, as usual, I had misjudged to the point of failure.

"Chocolates, how nice," she said. They were meant to be a nod of indifference to her growing weight, once a Bone of Contention. I used to call her awful names, screaming at her through the walls, ranting on about everything. But now that I had so publicly Straightened Out, I wanted to prove to everyone, including myself, that I wasn't that asshole any-more. I had changed. These chocolates, while cheap and unexceptional, were meant to be symbolic of something. But she was unimpressed.

"They're delicious," I told her.

"I'm sure they are. I *am* trying to lose weight, though."

"You don't need to. Really."

Her head tilted and I quickly shut up. I could see my past wash against her face, wearing away the character until only a smooth surface was left behind.

• • •

LUCKILY, things went much better with my son. "Two mitts," he shouted, holding one in each hand like a victorious boxer.

"Well, one's mine," I said.

"Which one?"

"The bigger one."

"Oh." He quickly relinquished my mitt, his face a bit disappointed at the sudden halfies of the score. But the web stitching, the loopy autograph, the red Raleigh patch quickly distracted him from feeling too gypped. He asked, "What's this say?"

"Ozzie Smith, one of the great fielding shortstops."

"Is he an Indian?"

"No, he's black." I glanced over at my wife, hoping to see some laugh lines at her eyes, but I don't think she even heard me. "Kidding," I said. "I think he plays for St. Louis."

"Who are they?"

"The Cardinals."

"What's that?"

"A bird, a red bird."

"Cool."

"Now What Do You Say?" his mother reminded, sucking the fun out of the moment.

"Oh. Thank You Very Much."

I almost reached out and ruffled his hair the way TV Fathers expressed affection for their TV Sons. *Leave It to Beaver, Bonanza, The Brady Bunch, The Cosby Show.* The history of TV can be traced through perfect families, though I often wondered why *The Honeymooners* didn't have any kids. Probably because Ralph Kramden would've been an abusive jerk.

"No problem," I said.

My heart panicked when he tried to force the mitt onto his left hand.

"Aren't you left-handed?" I said.

"Yep," he said.

"Well, the mitt goes on your right hand."

"Huh?"

I reached toward him. "Lefty means you throw with your left hand, catch with your right. You know that, don't you?"

"Sure."

"There, that's right," I said. "Now hold up your hand like you're catching a pop fly for the final out of the World Series."

I really should've gotten a ball as well. Two mitts and no ball. What could we do? Go out to the backyard and wave to each other? I tried to improvise by grabbing a section of the *Plain Dealer* and crumpling the paper into a makeshift ball. I lofted this creation at him, aiming for the pocket, but the leather was too stiff and the ball bounced off the mitt with the lightness of a rock on the moon.

"That was the TV listings," my wife told me.

"Oh," I said.

DURING dinner, after grace, the three of us found comfort in asking for things. "Please pass the peas," my son said. He was sitting on the baseball mitt—I had told him all of the hints on How to Break It In.

"Here you go."

"Pass the butter, please," my wife asked.

"Sure," I said. And after the first bite, I made a show of appreciation. "This is delicious, just delicious. How Do You Do It?"

She smiled.

"Pass the gravy." And the boy grinned when he said a long P-l-e-a-s-e.

I was at The Head of the Table, the facilitator of all passing, the slicer of Roast Beef. The conversation was minimal, centering mostly on food, but we luxuriated in this serenity.

We were travelers long delayed, finally coming to a hotel and calling it Home.

THE DISHES were left in the sink, the pots and pans soaking in sudsy water, my wife saying that She Would Wash Them Later.

"Are you sure?" I said. "Let me do them."

"That's all right."

But I started anyway, scraping the food into the garbage, running the faucet. I rolled up my sleeves and took hold of a bristled scrubber the shape of an old-fashioned microphone.

She was annoyed, her hands curling into fists and crossing her chest in a dead Pharaoh's pose. "You know we compost now. We don't just throw things out on a whim, we Consider the Mess." My wife had the perfect ability to speak in broad analogy.

"How long has that been going on?"

"A while. And please don't just let the water run, that's such a waste." She reached over and turned the gush into an icicle. "We Need to Conserve in This Day and Age."

"I hear you."

She watched me for a bit and then said, "Guess I might as well get the kid ready for bed."

It seemed too early for that, but I didn't say anything.

I MADE sure everything was spotless, even using the Brillo pads, though I hated the feel of them, the way I hated the feel of aluminum foil and newspapers and non-gloss paint on a wall. For some reason I could taste those things in my mouth, and that's all it took for me to gag.

Outside, the night turned the windows inward, and a few moths thumped against my reflection. They were desperate to get inside and flit around a lightbulb. I wondered what they did during the day. Lie low? Fly toward the sun? Or maybe they just slept off the glare of last evening.

• • •

My wife poked her head in. "You still at it?"

"Basically done."

"You didn't have to do that," she said. "But it's appreciated." She picked up a sponge and started to wipe down the countertop around the sink, sweeping the wet crumbs into her bare palm. Nothing made her squeamish; she had the constitution of a nurse.

"That Was Really a Great Dinner," I said.

"Thanks." She leaned against the refrigerator, a life-size magnet waiting for me to pick her off. "I'm Glad You're Here."

"Me Too."

"It's Nice."

"Yeah."

She smiled, shaking her head. "These are things to say."

"They sure are."

She unstuck herself to pour a glass of water. "You think you could paint the house?"

"Paint the house?"

"Yeah, it could use a fresh coat."

"I'm sure I could." The whole idea made me sick. "I'm no professional," I said to her. "I haven't painted a house since I was a kid."

"Just Fake It. You can do that."

"I suppose."

She told me to Go and Tuck the Boy In. When I got to his room, pausing at the door, I watched him read a durably made book. His expression was serious, as if the bed were a desk and the book a quarterly report and I the interrupting employee asking for a raise. "Good book?" I asked.

"Uh-huh."

"What's it about?"

"Well, it's about jobs, different kinds of jobs, a doctor, a policeman, a cook, those kinds of things."

I sat down next to him and looked over his shoulder. "Can you read now?"

"No, not yet. Sometimes, though."

"That's good."

He didn't answer.

"Would you like me to read to you?" I asked.

"That's all right."

"Okay."

Taped to the walls were pictures cut out of magazines, the edges raw with awkward scissoring. Most of them were lush photographs from *National Geographic*—a pride of lions, a herd of elephants, a group of elk—and I wondered if they should mean something to me, maybe a view into my son's mind, a puzzle of information a good father might be able to understand. Wildlife. Nature. No great realizations. Then I searched the room for other clues, but there weren't many around. Some art supplies. A couple of action figures. Toy cars and airplanes. In a wicker basket a few stuffed animals were having an orgy, the glass eyes of one teddy bear looking strung out and unable to comprehend How He Actually Got Here. "Where's your mitt?" I asked.

"Under the bed." The boy had his knees bent below his chin in a highly flexible display. He seemed to be all cartilage. If I had tried such a maneuver, I would've been sore for weeks.

"Where?" I said.

He tweaked a slight face—eyes widening, lips sucked in—which he didn't think I noticed. He leaned over the edge of his bed, his spine a hinge, the tops of his pajamas lifting to expose smooth white skin and a perfect crease of vertebrae. He surfaced with the mitt. "Like you said," he said.

"No no." I took the mitt from him. "Under the mattress, I said. It needs to get loose." I opened the pocket and dug my fist in there. "You really need some twine and a baseball and oil, then you've got the makings for a Job Well Done. What you do is sleep on it for a week, just sleep on it, maybe sometimes re-oiling, then you're ready. Makes a load of difference."

"To what?"

"To playing," I said. "You develop a pocket for the ball to fit into." I got up from the bed. "I really should've gotten you a ball. Fucking stupid of me."

"That's all right," my son said.

"It needs to be broken in properly. It's pretty important. Otherwise it's all crap." I paced the room. I have that habit, pacing, especially when I'm beginning a lie. I need to be on my feet and moving. "And you know what? I was going to save this, but you know what?"

He shook his head with slow deliberateness, even his shoulders turned.

"Well, this is a secret now, but I have opening-day tickets to the Indians game. I do. A friend snagged me a pair."

"Baseball?" the boy asked.

"Of course," I told him, now feeling alive with this story. "And good tickets. Third base line. Fourth row. The best. And the two of us are going. Have a great time. The two of us in Jacobs Field, that green grass, hot dogs, fucking banners waving, seventh-inning stretch, the whole deal, and we'll have our mitts because you never know when a foul ball might zip toward you. There's nothing more precious in the world. Nothing. People dive headfirst just for the opportunity to touch one. I swear. Practically kill themselves. And to catch one in a mitt, well, that's the greatest rush. Pull in a liner from Lofton or Belle, from Murray. Oh, man."

"Have you?"

"Not yet," I said. "But I'm waiting." My hands worked his tiny mitt. That leather smell was filled with the easy sentimentality of Baseball, of Fathers and Sons, of Hope, and my lie seemed to fit comfortably within that false promise of Spring. "We got to make you a pocket."

"A pocket?"

I slapped the inside of the mitt. "For the mitt, you know. Remember?"

"Oh yeah."

I reached into my jeans and scooped up my apartment keys and dropped them in the heel of the webbing, then for good measure I tucked my wallet in there too. "This'll barely do," I said.

"Looks good," my son said.

"Yeah?"

"Sure." His arms flopped at his sides with indifference.

"Okay." I reached down and took ahold of his mattress and lifted it to my chest. It was incredibly light. The boy rolled to the side, his body exaggerating the pitch, and he flattened himself against the wall. At first I was concerned that I had inadvertently hurt him, fears of The Night I Broke His Arm pushing against my temples, but right now he was laughing.

"Fun," he said.

"Yeah?"

"Yeah."

I placed the mitt in the center of the box spring and dropped the mattress down. He lurched to the other side, hitting my knees with a giggle. "Whoa," he said. "That's a ride."

"Earthquake," I shouted, and I started to fling the mattress around, but seeing him bounce all over the place put the Fear of God in me, so I stopped.

"C'mon, more."

"Nope," I said.

"Please."

"Nighttime."

He pawed at the bed like a cat. "I feel a something," he said.

"That's the mitt."

"Oh."

"But it does the job."

He said, "Okay," with a certain look, doubtful yet resigned, that I could've sworn belonged solely to me.

IN THE bedroom my wife had already changed into her nightgown and bathrobe, her hair combed out in feathered waves, and she smiled a smile of Home Again. "He all tucked in?"

"Yep."

"He asleep?"

"Not yet."

"Well," she said while rubbing moisturizer cream into her hands, the white disappearing within cracked fingers. "I'll go in and say good night. Be back in a sec."

Alone in the room, the bed seemed huge and the sheets seemed to glow and the pillows seemed to be arranged into a choir of comfort. Spend the Night, they sang. But I was feeling like a heathen and I eyed the window wondering about escape—if I would twist my ankle from the fall, if I could hobble to where I needed to go, if I could dodge this situation and find sanctuary.

"A BASEBALL game?" she asked.

"Yeah, I was thinking maybe."

"That'd be great. He's already excited." Her arms came around my neck, her pendant head hanging below me. "Will you stay?"

"I guess. Yeah, sure," I answered.

"I've Missed You," she said, and when someone says that to you, you only have one possible reply, and I said it.

WE MADE love. She handed me a condom before Things Went Too Far. "You never know," she said. It had been almost a year, and she was off the pill, and with my Dubious History she had every right to think that you never know. But for this rational behavior she apologized. "I'm sorry," she said. But I told her that I understood perfectly. "If it's a real bother," she said a few minutes later, "you can take it off, just be careful, pull out or something, you know, because this is so nice, it really is. I'm Very Happy." I held her wide face in my hands, my fingers massaging her scalp. She loved this. And I licked her neck because she loved that too. And I gave her deep kisses without tongue. And I made sure to hold my weight off her. I did those things with the inspiration of an actor reprising a tired role. Then I told her what she wanted to hear, wishing somehow that these words could be safe, that they could give pleasure without the fear of possible transmission.

SHE SLEPT draped over me, her leg in between my legs, her arm on my shoulder. Hot prickles of sweat developed where she touched me, an awful sensation, too clammy for my stomach, but I didn't want to move and disturb her. Just a year ago I would've kicked her to the other side of the bed. Outside, the moon was near full, bright enough to put shadows on the far wall. Cars passed. Once in a while a person walked on the sidewalk, the sex determined by the clicks of the shoes. Couples were louder, their voices drunk and in a certain turmoil. I listened to all of this. The occasional airplanes. The peel-outs. The mystery noises of Friday.

And I wished that this room had a TV. I'd sweep the volume way down so that some dialogue was lost, the soft words, the whispers, every conversation only partially understood, the secrets of plot left to the lip-readers. I'd try to find something worth watching, maybe a fine old movie I hadn't seen in a long time, any Hollywood classic where a damaged life is repaired and set back into motion. But all I had to distract me was the furniture, the bureau with silos of makeup, the chair with my clothes draped over the back, the closet door half opened as if someone were spying from there, checking out this diorama, a temporary display in a museum of natural history. This Is How They Lived. This Is the World Unspoiled. The background painted. The lighting blue nocturnal. The taxidermist doing an expert job of covering up the fatal bullet holes, the scratching and clawing of bloody instinct into a Pose of Tranquillity for the Dead Zoo. But my fingernails were clumped up with family.

"Are you awake?" my wife whispered.

The person peeking from the closet would see that I didn't answer but breathed a bit harder as if I were deep in sleep and couldn't hear her. Maybe she would give up and let me pretend for a while longer that I was the Recovered Husband, that I was the Returned Father to the son down the hall, my keys and wallet safely under his mattress, his dreaming body above them, rising and falling, breaking in the mitt with his own weight.

She rubbed my shoulder. "Are You Awake, Honey?" she asked again.

Don't Go
in
the
Basement!

THERE'S GOING TO be a noise, a thwumping noise from the basement, a hollow noise that sounds every few seconds—thwump, pause, pause, thwump—as if a clock is keeping time for a madman, and I'll hear this noise from the kitchen, my wet body wrapped in a bathrobe, my skin flushed with recent sex, and I'll look long and hard at the basement door, at the doorknob in particular, and I'll tentatively call out Chip's name—"Chip, you down there?"—but there will be no answer except for that noise—thwump, pause, pause, thwump—so I'll question that noise again—"Chip, is that you?"—before opening the basement door, pressing my palm against its brassy reflection.

This overhanging certainty frightens me, the same way final exams frighten me on the first day of classes. It is part of a non-mystical future, the nuts and bolts of a syllabus, inescapable until the end. My sorority sisters consider me a fatalist of the worst kind, a person who sees herself in the alcoholic form of her mother, who composes a eulogy for her father whenever she's with him on holidays. The problem is that I lack the calm acceptance of a true fatalist. Instead, I'm simply impatient while I wait for the statistics to kick in.

Someone screams, "Sally!"

"Yes."

"Are you coming, or what?"

"Or what," I say.

"Suit yourself." And they're gone, my sisters, the sisters of Kappa Kappa Gamma, all thirty-seven sisters marching in menstrual-cycle sync across the lush lawns of Greek Way. I watch them from my upstairs window, the twenty-two with boyfriends, the nineteen with the same favorite song, the fifteen with eating disorders, the eleven with cocaine desires, the nine with drinking problems, the seven with secret abortions, the five on antidepressants, the one with unfortunate acne. These shared numbers shift from day to day in what are public and often cruel exchanges, but tonight they are a union of desperate girls off to the Saturday Night Homebrew Bash at Sigma Phi Epsilon. T-shirts and blue plastic mugs have been manufactured, as well as beer, all types fermented in the basements of sororities and fraternities: ΔΥ "on your ass" amber, ΦM "you'll be stewed" heiferweizen, ΦKA "lights out" stout, XΩ "see you later" lager, TKE "pukin' in the john" porter, AKA "47" malt liquor.

The sisters carry six-packs of KKΓ "I wanna scama" pilsner, like young executives with their briefcases swinging. Off to work they go. In five hours, at two in the morning, those remaining at the ΣΦE house, the girls without boyfriends, the girls without one night stands, the girls without cocaine, the girls without mysterious blackouts, those defeated girls will slouch back to this house, the party sweat now bitterly freezing on their skin, and they'll wash up and slip on their nightgowns in the silence of the drunkenly unloved. Luckily, there will be no time for them to think before they pass out.

The clock radio on my bedside table glows a blue 9:37 P.M., the numbers shifting like the numbers of some dyslexic countdown. Often, in the morning, I'll wake up just a few minutes before the alarm beeps, and I'll lie there within the safe sheets and track the maneuvering of those stick-figure numbers. I'll try to tick off the seconds in my head, to test my internal timekeeping ability, but I'm always a few seconds short or a few seconds long, and though I'm ready for t-minus zero to hit, the alarm nonetheless startles me, as if my life will simply end at that moment.

At 9:40 P.M., the girlish echoes are gone, and I get up from the bed. But before I can make one step toward the bureau mirror and its critical reflection, a hand shoots out from under the paisley dust ruffle and grabs me by the left ankle. I immediately let out a high-pitched scream, but it combines with the other outside noises. On Saturday night no one can differentiate between the levels of hysteria. With a sharp tug the hand pulls me to the floor, face first, so that my arms are stretched forward like a failed Superman, and before I can start some defensive kicking, the other hand has control of my right leg. A body quickly climbs up my backside, knees pinning my legs, elbows pinning my arms; a chin digs into my neck. I can't believe this is just one person, it feels like a small army of well-trained limbs. There's no way I can move. A groin grinds my ass. A tongue licks the smooth heel of my ear. The realization—I will be raped—doesn't really shock me. In fact, I can't believe it's taken this long for something violent and awful to happen to me. A nose greedily snorts my odor.

In a few long instants I imagine the aftermath: the call to the police, the trip to the hospital, the I've-seen-it-all nurse taking Polaroids to document the assault. It will be difficult to find the suspect, almost impossible, and even if they do find him, in a bar, a scratch across his face, the telltale tattoo on his biceps, the case will be hard to prosecute. Where's the evidence? No semen, no fingerprints, no positive ID—my rapist is a smart rapist and he will have worn a condom and gloves and a ski mask. So I'll have to take the stand in that dusty courtroom, the old judge looking at me like he's my shamed father, while my kindly lawyer guides me through the horrendous incident, and the cruel defense lawyer, his face pitted with vindictive pockmarks, bullies me into revealing my sordid sex life. Do I have to remind you, Sally, that you are under oath?

A voice whispers hotly, "I'm going to fuck you."

"What?"

"Right here, right now. If you move, I'll kill you. I swear."

"Chip?"

"Shut up, bitch! I have a knife."

I stare at the hands holding me and try to notice something Chip-ish about them: a scar on the index finger, gnawed hangnails, cracked skin. But the attacker has on wool mittens with a Nordic design. "Chip, is that you, you idiot?"

"C'mon, shut up." I can hear the conspicuous wavering in his voice, that little boy not yet released from uncertainty. At times—watching TV, brushing his teeth, blowing his nose—you can spot the young Chip, cowlick and freckles, wearing his brother's hand-me-downs. He still gets excited about fresh-baked cookies. And while I once envisioned myself going out with older guys, the upperclassmen of this world, I found freshman Chip in History 203, his feet kicking the seat in front of him, my seat.

"Excuse me?" I said, and I turned around and gave him an annoyed aura perfected by four years of high school and two years of college.

"Yes."

"Stop kicking." And he stopped just like that. "Thank you," I said, and I faced forward again and watched the professor try to explain the causes of World War II to an auditorium of three hundred students. But Chip's face stuck with me, something about the crooked smile, the misshapen hair, the bemused eyes, and while I listened to the tragic consequences of a passive public, I couldn't get the guy out of my head. What was he doing right now? Taking fastidious notes or sleeping or gazing around the room or doodling? My insides had that shaken feeling of an accident narrowly avoided.

"Chip, get the hell off of me."

The body slowly rolls to the side, coming to rest on his back, defeated like an animal confronting the alpha of the species.

"Take off that stupid ski mask."

Chip pulls it free, creating a static mess. He's very sweaty, breathing hard, thin not from athletics but from of a highly motivated metabolism. He's wearing a blue jogging outfit, Adidas, circa 1978.

"How long have you been under my bed?"

"Three hours."

"Jesus, that's creepy. All that time."

"Fucking hot."

I reach over and punch him in the stomach, hitting him in the place my father calls the breadbasket. It makes him grunt and fold. "So is this your idea of a romantic Saturday night, you idiot?"

"What?"

"A little raping, you sentimental fool."

"Give me a break."

I slap him a good one across the face, catching him with the bone of my wrist.

"Jesus, you cut me," he says, dabbing his lip for blood.

"Oh, poor baby." I lean over him, a carrion-eating vision of beauty, and give him a tongue-loaded kiss. He tastes like an eight volt battery.

"You're crazy," he says after I have my fill. "All this outrage for something you suggested." His voice shrills into the international parody of a bitchy woman. " 'Hey, Chip, wouldn't it be a kick to play out a rape thing, you know, a fantasy of some sorts. Maybe you could do that sometime, surprise me.' That's what you said, don't try to deny it; you practically scripted it for me."

"I didn't expect you to take to it with so much vigor."

"Hell, I didn't want to do it in the first place. Freaked me out."

I straddle his chest, my knees on his arms, my hands on his sternum. "There's some awful statistic that one out of three women are raped in this country. Isn't that unbelievable? When I heard that I was shocked, really shocked."

"It's awful," he says.

"Is this what your older brother used to do? Pin you down and make you eat his spit?" A strand of saliva inches from my mouth, growing longer and thinner, the tension approaching terminal elasticity before I suck it back in.

"Don't you dare."

"Repressed memories, huh?" I make a fist, knuckling my middle finger for a noogie kill. "How about drilling for oil; did he do that?"

"I can flip you when I want."

I start to tunnel on his sternum, and true to his word, he rolls me. Now he's on top of me. "All I have to do is grab your balls," I tell him. "I couldn't stand going through life with such a blatant piece of vulnerability. There for the taking. A bull's-eye."

"You have to give birth" is his lame retort.

"That's all by choice, honey. Besides, my uterus is so screwed up that there's no chance. My contraceptive is all natural."

He eases up on his grip. "I thought you were on the pill," he says.

"No, no; I said I was a pill."

"Funny."

"I try."

"You should've told me. Something I'd like to know." He gets up and leans against a wall, his face an expression of supposed caring. "I mean, that's harsh, that's really harsh."

"Trust me, it's not. It's simply a fact. And please don't

look at me like this is some revealed secret, it's just scarred ovaries." I'm on my feet now, brushing my thighs, pulling my hair back and tying it with an elastic. "I swear to God, you boys watch too many soap operas."

He takes off his mittens and drops them on the bed, looking like a surgeon after he's lost a patient. "I don't know about you," he tells me.

"You have an inkling."

"I really don't." He unzips the top of the jogging suit, revealing a white triangle of T-shirt.

"But you're smitten anyway."

"Maybe."

"The danger," I say.

"The what?"

"The danger."

He heels off his shoes and flicks them into the corner. "Oh yeah, I forgot."

Outside cars rev by, their mufflers purposefully destroyed to create a distinctive sound of approach, the owners christening them The Beast and The Land Shark and T-Rex. They cruise around with an accompaniment of bass-laden music, mostly hip-hop though occasionally the windows shake with Led Zeppelin. And tonight there seems to be an abundance of fireworks on campus, a rural approximation of urban gunfire.

"So," I say.

"So," Chip parrots back.

I go over and sit on the bed next to him and call him "My little baby freshman."

He answers with "My over-the-hill junior."

"My boy toy."

"My hag rag."

Then I ask him, "Would you ever hurt me?"

"Huh?"

"You know, hit me or something."

He touches his lip. "If I remember correctly, you're the one who hit me."

"You were raping me."

"I was doing what you asked me to do a couple of days ago."

"I wasn't serious."

"Oh, please," he says.

"I was thinking out loud."

"Just stop it," he says.

"You certainly took to it naturally."

"What is this?"

"I'm just wondering if you could ever get mad enough to hit me, that's all."

"No. Never. What do you think?"

"One in three women get abused by their husbands."

"Everything is one and three with you. I don't think you even have the right numbers," he says.

"So you question the validity of my statement?"

"No. I only question the validity of you," he says.

"That's sexist."

He stands up and walks toward the door. "I'm not going to play this game. It's tiring."

"So you're tired of me. Just up and leave when you're tired of me. It's just that simple. Married for twenty years, three kids, and one day, 'Hmm, this is a bit dull, so good-bye.' Is that what you're implying?"

"What are you saying?" He smiles an uncontainable smile, a smile for the humorously unwell.

I ask him, "Are you having an affair? Have you lost all of our money? Are you molesting the kids? Do you have terminal cancer?"

"Yes. No. No. And it's a distinct possibility."

I get up and go over to him and place my hands on his hips and squeeze and ingratiate myself with his groin. "That's what I love about you," I say. "You think fast."

"Whatever you say."

"I say we go to Katrina's room."

"Is she next?" he asks.

"She sure is."

We walk down the hall, impressionist posters on either side of us, mostly Monet and his lame garden, the blues and greens, the bridge, the water lilies; then there are a couple of Renoirs, the girls playing piano, the girls bathing, plump and pasteled, their beauty soft and non-threatening. Renoir sucks. And Monet isn't much better. But the girls of Greek Way love them, this Martha Stewart version of art. We stop at Katrina's door with its erasable message board, a palimpsest of different colored inks leaving behind the news of a visit—*Hey Kat, stopped by, guess you're out, talk to you, Laura*—and the schedule of the occupant's night—*At Sig Ep to party!* I pick up the tethered Magic Marker and pop off the top and write *Cuntrina* in big red letters.

"Jesus," Chip says, laughing.

I surround my portmanteau with hearts and daisies, with the faces of geometrical dogs I learned how to make in third grade. I open the door. No one bothers with locks at Kappa Kappa Gamma. "Shall we?"

"Sure."

Katrina, the senior, the vice president of the sorority, the hayseed debutante, the cocaine whore, the occasional slut, the straight-A student, the majestically unbeautiful but always loved, has one of the seven singles in the house and I hate her for it. The walls of her room are plastered with cutouts of advertisements: men in underwear, men in fine Italian suits, men playing volleyball, their squinted eyes staring into the center of the room. Her well-intentioned bed is piled with a pyramid of comfy pillows. Strewn on the floor is the chrysalis of a jogging outfit: a support bra, Lycra tights, a terry-cloth headband, blue anklets, Nike cross-trainers. Makeup inhabits the top of her bureau like a futuristic city, and the sock drawer sticks out with the impunity of a brat's tongue. The closet door is open, the light left on, and a variety of outfits hang there with a Cinderella melancholy.

"Well," Chips says seconds before he plops down on the bed. "How many more after this?"

"Seven," I tell him. "At least I think it's seven."

"And what'll we do after that?"

"Who knows?" For the last month we've been having sex in each room of the house, fifteen rooms to date—ten doubles, five singles—though we haven't tackled the living room or the dining room or the kitchen. But that wasn't part of the deal. The plan just mapped out bedrooms, the private space of my fellow sisters, and me the spy to their world, their sheets, their clothes, their desires. I am collecting evidence, researching histories, crunching the numbers, the data of their dreams, and Chip finds all this extremely sexy, but then again he'd find dark missionary love sexy as well.

"We're going to get caught at some point," he says. I can tell he wants to show me something unsurprising in his pants. He's practically squirming on the bed.

"No doubt," I say. I turn toward the closet and run my hands through Katrina's things: summer dresses, short black skirts, Indian print blouses, almost the same exact wardrobe as the other fifteen closets. "And we will be burned at the stake," I add.

"They could have a party," he says. "A Joan the Arc party."

"Of," I say.

"Huh?"

"Nothing." I've picked out a dress, what looks like an old prom dress with taffeta and chiffon and fine lacework. I hold it against myself. "How's this, darling?"

"Fab," he says.

I turn around and slip out of my sweats—Chips oohs like it's the Fourth of July—and step into the dress. Though Katrina is smaller than I am by a good four inches, I still manage to squeeze into the contraption, the crinoline high on my thighs. I twirl and say, "Will you marry me?"

"Oh, Katrina," Chip replies, his eyes dewy.

"Because I think I'm pregnant."

"I don't care."

I skip toward him. "That's why I love you. You're going to be such a good father."

"I'll try."

I slide off his jogging pants. The elastic of his jockeys catches on his hard-on, and when finally freed, his dick slaps against his stomach like a foot stepping down on a puddle. Already his hips are gyrating, and his mouth is grimaced in porn-star heat, and his arms are held outward, ready to be filled with my approaching body. Seeing this, it's hard to respect a man.

"Calm down," I say.

"What?"

"You're so . . . never mind."

I mount him—I love that word, "mount," so imperial, so portentous, to mount, very popular in romance novels, she mounts this, she mounts that, it's the only active fuck-verb for a woman, mount mount mount mount mount, I swear, I could say it forever—and Chip groans and tells me that I feel so good, and I look down on him from my kneeling position glad that his eyes are closed because I have a smile on my face. Just a little one. A mounting smile.

"Chip?"

"Yeah?" His eyes open but they hold a creased need, like a boy who has to go to the bathroom but can't find Mommy.

"What would you do if I was pregnant?"

"Huh?"

"Well, I'm late."

"Late?"

"Yeah. Five weeks."

His body freezes in mid-thrust. "Five weeks!" I feel his erection subside within me. Penile introspection. I imagine the blood rushing to the panicky heart. "But you said your ovaries are not right, you said you were on the pill, you said, well, it was taken care of."

"That's what I thought. I guess you have stubborn sperm." I reach behind and cup his testicles; the scrotum is shrink-wrapped around his walnuts. "You must have a bunch of engineers in there."

"But five weeks? Why didn't you say something?"

"Sometimes I just miss my period. I'm not regular."

"Huh? Wait a second. Are you Katrina right now or Sally?"

"I'm Sally, stupid."

"Come on, you're fucking with me."

"Well, I'm trying to fuck you, but you're like some old man, you thirty years from now, impotent with a pregnant lover while your wife is drunk at home with the kids."

Chip wiggles out from beneath the crinoline. "This isn't funny, you know, this whole thing, getting tired. Like the HIV thing."

"That was a legitimate fear."

"The seizures."

"Do you want to talk to the doctor?"

"I don't know. And when do I know?"

"Not until the game's over." I stand up and step out of the dress and toss it into the bottom of the closet. My skin is itchy from the synthetic material.

"So," Chip says. "Is this legit, this I'm-pregnant deal?"

I put my hands on my hips because I can't resist such a pose. "What do you think?"

"No," he says.

"Then no it is." I walk toward the door. "I'm taking a shower. You're welcome to join me, especially if your flaccid little friend feels like playing."

From behind I hear him mutter something about Demi Moore and Sharon Stone. I don't mind the comparison. I can handle it. And as the warm water from the shower slides down my body, I think of the history of obligatory shower scenes, the perfect opportunity to show some tit and ass, from slasher flicks to prestige films, the ideal mesh between the dirty and the clean, and as I lather up, moving the soap along my long legs—Foal was the nickname my father gave me—Chip appears and begins washing my hair, his fingers massaging my scalp, suds raising then falling down my face, always a vulnerable situation, that childhood fear of getting soap in your eyes, the endless stinging, the implied danger of a blinding incident, and as I squeeze my lids tight, Chip fumbles his way inside of me, hopeless until I guide him in.

"Mmmmmm," he says, as if I'm a hamburger in a commercial.

"Who wrote this dialogue?"

"Hmm?"

"Nothing," I tell him. "It's just that you feel so good. Yes. So good. Oh, fuck me. Yes. Like that. There. Yes. Ahh. Cock hard. Yes. Good." Sexual conversation is the equivalent of talking to a foreigner; words are often repeated, verbs are dumped for the charade of movement, and understanding is feigned with a smile. "Harder. You. Yes. You fuck. Good." This, of course, makes him come in a second, and I play along, a performance worthy for an audience of more than one.

"That was nice," Chip tells me, his body leaning against tile. When his hair is wet, you can see his impending baldness, and you can tell it won't be a graceful exit. He doesn't have the head for it. "Really," he says. "Great."

"Sure," I answer.

"Wasn't it?" he says. "I mean, yeah."

I say, "Fine," knowing that this word kills him.

"Fine?"

"Yeah." And now that I have him thinking, I touch his face and say, "Fine is good."

"Fine is. Well, fine. It's just. Kind of. The thing is." He stammers like a method actor. "You fucking with me again?"

I turn off the water and sweep aside the shower curtain as if an opening night ovation awaits me on the other side. "I'm getting a little sick of that question. All of a sudden, that's all you can say." My voice deepens into the international parody of an oafish man. " 'Are you fucking with me? Is this a joke? Duh, what's going on?' Jesus, get a clue."

Chip is upset. "Where are the fucking towels?"

"In my room."

"No towels in here?"

"No. You'll have to brave the wilds of the hall, big man."

Before leaving he turns around and says, "It's just that I like you. Okay?"

My reply devastates. "That's sweet," I tell him. "Really sweet."

I linger in the bathroom, letting Chip stew on his own, even though I'm starting to feel cold. The heat in the house has been turned off early this year because of the eco-conscious Libby Plower and her whole Greekology movement. Recycling, composting, conserving, letter-writing, protesting, campaigning, raising consciousness, all that crap. Under the direction of Ms. Plow-me—Chip and I fucked in her room about two weeks ago; I wore her "Earth Day '95" T-shirt—the girls of Kap Gam go out every other Saturday and clean up a three-mile stretch of highway, a good mix of environmental concerns and community needs. As if this will make a difference, as if anything will make a difference. Save the world. No chance. All you're doing is setting yourself up for disappointment, for tears when the last elephant is killed, for heartbreak when the seas become oil, so much emotional energy wasted on the inevitable.

The door opens. This frightens me, but it's only Chip, and he throws me my bathrobe and says, "Here. I'm going downstairs."

"Okay."

"See ya."

I wrap myself in terry, loving the feel of that fabric, rough yet soft, and I rub myself in order to dry off, arms crossing over my torso like I'm a madwoman in the bathrobe version of a straitjacket. After showers, I always find myself thinking about cutting my hair, chopping it all off and not bothering with hair dryers and not fearing frizziness and not worrying about how long it would take to grow back out. But these are just crazy thoughts. Through the frosted window the red and white of a passing police car flashes by, though there is no accompanying siren, the emergency not that desperate, probably student-oriented. This is a safe place. This is a safe college town. I pull tight the sash and tie a loose bow, and feeling thirsty, I make my way to the kitchen to get a glass of water.

The stairs creak.

"Hey, Chip," I call out.

Nothing. Maybe he left.

"Chip, listen, I'm sorry." I play the word "sorry," trilling the syllables.

I open the fridge. The special items—the wheat germ, the fancy juice, the French grain mustard—have Post-it Notes stuck to them with the names of the purchasers. They wave at me, pleading for someone to save them from their anal owners. I start to sing, "How do you solve a problem like Maria?" a song I learned when I was ten and elbowed at the TV in my parents' living room. My mother used to love to perform the opening montage of *The Sound of Music,* her body spinning, her balance drunken, her arms making a mess of any precious thing. She was more of a tornado than a nun. And my father would change the words to Mr. Von

Trapp's heart-wrenching anthem, crooning "Addled Vice" with just the right amount of bathos.

There's a noise—the noise I've been expecting, the thwump, pause, pause, thwump noise—coming from the basement.

"Chip, you down there?"

I step toward the door, as if closeness will reveal something.

"Chip, is that you?"

I know, I know, only a moron would go down into the basement. In all of those slasher movies, the girl in peril—the cute coed alone at the sorority, simply a number in a growing body count—is found posed in some god-awful way, hanging upside down with her throat cut, a tableau of death for the last living sorority sister to run into as she flees the maniac. And you, the knowing audience, scream at the screen, "No! Don't be so stupid! Don't you realize what will happen?" And you turn to your friends and say, "That's so ridiculous. Who would do that? I'd run out of the house, stark naked if I had to." And, of course, you'd be saved, and you'd graduate, and you'd find your place in this world, but years later, you'd be left with the emptiness of your survival, the nolo contendere of such instincts. Whom did you leave behind? Trust me, there will be someone.

I reach for the knob to the basement door, my palm pressing against its brassy reflection. FDR had it all wrong. Nowadays, we have nothing but fear, just the fear itself, to sustain a sense of fleeting reality, and the days and nights of infamy loom ahead with bright-eyed appeal.

CPR

IT WAS THE winter of phantom heart attacks. While Paul slept, Kate listened to his breathing, his snores, his wet tasting of dreams, and she'd wait for an unfamiliar sound to destroy, suddenly, the rhythm. What was that? And she'd roll over and watch the sheets over his chest, watch his face for any signs of pain. A grimace. A scowl. She could almost see him on the gurney in the hospital morgue, just his head exposed for her identification. "Yes, that's him," she'd say, "that's my husband," and the doctor would nod and cover him and slide him back into that human filing cabinet. Kate would begin to feel sick at the prospect of sleeping with a corpse, of waking up with cold flesh at her side—blue lips, dry eyes—so she'd pay close attention to Paul, waiting for something to happen. Those moments were like the initial moments after an airplane's takeoff, when landing gear retracts and flaps grind and engines throttle. But soon, Paul's disruption would fade into a smooth flight, and Kate would feel silly for worrying. He might not have been in the greatest shape, smoking a pack a day and eating recklessly, but he was only fifty-six and had no history of heart disease. Still, it was a wary age, too young to die but too old to qualify as a tragedy.

During the day, at home, Kate often found herself ready

for that awful phone call, her hand reluctant to answer. "Yes, hello." Most probably it'd be Jack, his law partner for the past twenty years. He'd be in tears because he's an emotional man, unlike Paul, who can be rather distant and aloof. Jack would say, "Kate . . . oh God . . . I don't . . . I have . . . there's something . . ." his baffled tongue unable to form the words, but by then she'd understand everything. It might happen at his desk as he ate a hot dog slathered with sauerkraut, or maybe on the elevator as he cursed the slowly ticking floors. Grabbing his left arm, Paul would whiten and his skin would crumple. A massive coronary. He'd hit the ground beyond saving, though a young paralegal would try reviving him. At the funeral everyone would be shocked but not surprised, the same way divorce and a child's drug addiction don't seem to carry the same weight as they once did.

But Kate also had another variation on her husband's heart attack. This time the two of them are together, and they're walking on the beach even though they never walk on the beach anymore. Too sandy, Paul usually tells her. But today he relents because he's in an unexpectedly romantic mood, and they're holding hands and allowing the cold water to wash past their bare ankles and blot their rolled-up pants. Kate's not sentimental enough to see this happening during a sunset, but it's a surprising day, the sun warm and the air cold and the beach empty of people. They are both happy. Paul is singing made-up songs and occasionally turns her under his arm. He kisses her fingers. He talks about retiring. He calls her "Late" with affection. And Kate's at ease knowing that he's at ease, her temperament conditioned to his state of mind. Paul stops and steps away, his foot ready to kick water at her, and then it happens. He collapses. For a second Kate thinks that he's joking, but he's not much of a physical comedian. "Paul, what's wrong?"

He can't speak.

She kneels down next to him, her pants getting soaked. He looks like a sky diver whose chute hasn't opened, his arms and legs spread out in free-fall despair. "What is it?" Kate says rather pitifully. Then a large wave, the first of a set, pushes the tide past them.

She starts screaming—"Someone, please!"—destroying her vocal chords in a single burst. "Help me!" comes out raw.

The million-dollar beach houses have their shades drawn, their furniture wrapped in plastic, their hi-tech alarms armed for intruders—this is the off-season on Long Island, where the week and the weekend exist peacefully together. But right now Kate would kill for time-share crowds. Paul musters the strength to speak three letters. "CPR," he says.

CPR? She has no idea how to do that, only a vague notion from doctors on television. So she fakes it as well as possible, pounding on his chest, then blowing in his mouth. The salt water splashed on his lips has an almost sexual taste. And now the waves are really rolling in. And while Kate struggles to resuscitate him, she realizes that she's performing the antithesis of that famous scene in *From Here to Eternity,* where Burt Lancaster and Deborah Kerr are swept away with passion. Kate was twelve years old when she saw that movie, and in that lush theater, the walls ornate, the seats rich velvet, a group of girls giggled with an uncertain knowledge, and they leaned into each other and grazed shoulders and felt the excitement of the coming years, its certainty as thrilling as the crashing surf.

IN February, Kate decided to go to the American Red Cross for a basic course on lifesaving skills. They called it Community CPR, a term she liked. It brought to mind a giant hand descending onto Central Park, onto the arrested Great Lawn, and huge lips giving mouth-to-mouth to the frozen reservoir. This made her think of spring, and spring was her eventful season. She was born on April 25. She was married on May 18. She gave birth to Jeannie on May 3, to Sarah on June 6. Funny how it works that way. But what that also means is that winter is a season of annoying incubation. Her mother was laid up in bed for the final trimester, and she pointed to stretch marks as if they were wounds from a war. "You were an impossible fetus," she often said. The months before Kate's wedding were filled with screaming matches about the ever-expanding guest list, mutterings on the royal cost, and an overall sense of doom that struck Paul in mid-January and hobbled him with a heavy sense of fate. He took to saying, "Oh, well," in the face of everything. The pregnancy with Jeannie was nerve-racking, as all first pregnancies are, and when Kate became large, she was scared of stairs and ice and rushing pedestrians and overly excited dogs. The second pregnancy was less tense but more exhausting. Jeannie, three years old, discovered the joy of running, and Sarah managed to give Kate the worst heartburn of her life. So, as a result of all the joy in her life, Kate is not a winter person.

She made her way down Amsterdam Avenue. Two inches of snow had fallen the night before, enough to make the streets tricky and to bring out men with shovels who scraped toward the curb and sprinkled rock salt as if it were chicken feed. Kate went up the steps of the American Red Cross Center, a stocky building of glass and concrete. Inside the lobby, she unbuttoned her coat and stepped hard with her boots, leaving behind replicas of tread. A black woman behind a desk stared long and hard at this performance, her head angled with possible displeasure. Kate asked, "Have I made a mess?"

"Huh?" the woman said.

"The snow." Kate glanced over at what had been tracked in.

"Ask the janitor. His problem, not mine."

Kate told her, "I'm here for the CPR course."

"Name?"

"Kate Gerard."

The woman consulted a list, and then said, "Third floor, room 308."

"Thank you."

"You're very welcome." Kate couldn't tell if this woman was being polite or rude, an unsure feeling she has with minorities, an unfortunate feeling of being a fool, of not understanding the obvious, an unwelcome feeling that also lingers when she's with her husband and daughters—it's as if she's to blame for something basic and undeniable and forever ensnared in history. But these are the people you love.

Kate walked over to the bank of elevators.

ROOM 308 was at the end of the hall, the last room on the left, behind a heavy door with a small window reinforced with wire. Kate peeked in before entering. Under her winter coat were jeans and a white sweatshirt, a pair of Treetorn sneakers in her shoulder bag. This is an outfit she usually wears while gardening, but it seemed appropriate for the matter at hand, pliant for bending and loose enough to allow easy movement of the arms, the stretching and extending of hard work. To be honest, she's happiest in these clothes, though Paul would've asked, "Why so dumpy?" if he had seen her leave this morning. But he was already at work, probably on his fifth cup of coffee and third danish, unaware of her plans today.

Kate pushed through the door, and nine faces glanced up from five tables. They were mostly women, mostly women of color, from very black to almost white, mostly younger by thirty years; the lone man, more of a boy in his late teens, sat in the corner and played a handheld computer game, his torso swaying with pursuit. Standing there, Kate felt like the new student from a different country. She slipped toward the back, to a table where a brown woman hunched over a book of crossword puzzles. Kate smiled and pulled out a seat and draped her coat on the backrest and changed into sneakers and arranged her boots and checked her wristwatch and wished that she had other distractions to shrink the distance of waiting. This study-hall atmosphere almost put her in the mood to hunker down and scrawl a mash note to the boy in the second row—*I think you're cute*—and ball it up and toss it toward him. Early on in their courtship, when Paul was in the army and Kate was at school in Switzerland, she did little but ski and plump up on an accent-perfect pronunciation of "pain au chocolate" and write sappy letters to Sergeant Gerard. They always began with "Darling" and ended with "Forever Kate," the paragraphs in between scripted with hope for a future life together. When Jeannie found them stashed in a manila envelope—she was tripping around the attic a couple of months ago on her Christmas visit from California—she brought them down to her mother and said, "Guess what I've found?" like a bratty girl who knows your embarrassing secret.

"What?" Kate asked.

She rode out the tease, "Love letters," then emptied them on the kitchen table, the thin blue paper at once recognizable. Jeannie said, "I feel like I'm a character in that stupid *Bridges of Madison County,* but instead of studboy, whatever his name, I've uncovered a secret affair you had with Dad."

"I didn't read the book," Kate told her with a certain amount of pride.

"Mom, these letters, these letters are, well, they're so . . ." Jeannie smiled with postgraduate attitude. "The definition of the banality of love," she said.

"I was nineteen years old." Kate picked up a random letter. She hadn't seen them in decades, long forgotten in storage. The handwriting looked more youthful, and this surprised her, that even handwriting aged.

"Oh, I don't mean to be harsh," claimed Jeannie. "It's just, well, it's cute, that's all. But hey, did Dad ever write back?"

"Sure he wrote back," Kate answered, spreading the sheets in Go Fish fashion. "They should be in here as well."

"Trust me, they're not."

UP FRONT, on the floor of the classroom, the practice manikins were laid out like the victims of a Greek tragedy: the fathers, identical in red jogging suits, beside their sons, identical in shorts and American Red Cross T-shirts, beside their baby brothers, identical in duct-taped diapers. Kate imagined that somewhere, probably hidden in a basement closet, the rubber Medeas were stacked.

Baseboard heaters clicked with fresh helpings of heat, and fluorescent lights droned above, and bass-loaded music leaked from headphones, and a few coughs ripped through unwell lungs. "Jesus," the woman next to Kate said, her quick pigeon eyes searching out the person. "I've been warned about that."

Kate took this as an invitation to talk. "About what?" she asked.

The woman studied Kate as if she were a clue in the puzzle book. "Easy to catch something here. Everyone putting their tongues on the dummies."

"They must clean them," Kate said.

"I'm sure they'll tell you that they scrub them down and disinfect them, but who's got time and who's going to know and all that while I'm sick in bed and missing work because I sucked face with a nasty dummy." This woman's wide face displayed a fondness for conspiracy—her forehead sloped, her lips a purse of intrigue—but it also held the broad attributes of a sense of humor. "I'm serious," she said, half laughing.

"Kind of like cooties."

"Cooties?"

"Boy germs."

"That's right," she said. "This is cooties central."

The door opened, and the two of them quickly hushed, and ten faces glanced up for the impending entrance. A man walked in carrying the bulky briefcase of a traveling salesman. "Sorry I'm late," he said. He put the briefcase down on the desk and freed the latches and began pulling things out with a certain discipline—making piles, arranging papers. Kate saw him as a poor relative from the gourd family, tapered from head to toe, a squash of ugly flesh recently snatched from the dirt. This unfortunate physique was made even worse by a bald scalp dented with hollows and a pair of black-rimmed glasses and an adenoidal voice flecked with the odor of loam and sharp hair sprouting from his ears and nostrils, a tuft of it poking from the collar of his shirt, which held the half-moon watering of underarm perspiration.

"My name is Norman Churlick, and I'm your instructor today." He hitched up his pants—the first of many hitches; and picked at his groin—the first of many picks; and wiped at the milky corners of his lips—the first of many wipes. "Now let's take roll and pay fees and get on with it."

KATE THUMBED through the American Red Cross Community CPR Workbook. Its cover had a photograph of a man executing picture-perfect chest compressions on a waitress in a diner. Other customers watched with the appropriate expressions of panic. Decorations alluded to the Christmas season. This entire tableau seemed to intimate the salvaged middle of a story, a still photo from a medical Movie of the Week. And inside the book, at each chapter heading, other photographs illustrated the lessons to be learned: an infant not breathing, an infant choking, an infant having a heart attack; a child not breathing, a child choking, a child having a heart attack; an adult not breathing, an adult choking, an adult having a heart attack. But again, there were stories here. The man not breathing was at a summer pool party.

The boy in all three of the child chapters wore an Indian outfit—dress-up gone horribly wrong. The baby girl happily eating grapes didn't know that once the page was turned a grape would be lodged in her windpipe. All these brief scenes, and when Kate began to look closer, she started to recognize the people from picture to picture. The businessman choking was a father having a heart attack was a Good Samaritan giving mouth-to-mouth. The waitress near dead was the supermom to the troublesome boy was a wife to the drowned man. There was an interconnectedness in this small town on the edge of death, where everyone was a part of everyone else and together they saved each other in what were almost daily exchanges of breath. And the dying infant would grow into the dying child who would grow into the dying adult.

Norman gave the class a brief lecture on the goals of the course, on his training, on the requirements to pass; then he discussed the manikins, their proper care, and their sanitary guidelines. "After each use," he told them, "wipe the face down with rubbing alcohol. And if anyone is sick right now, or has an infectious disease, or cuts around the mouth, well, they should make themselves known to me." No hands raised. "I should stress," Norman continued, "that the risk of any kind of disease transmission during CPR training is extremely low. Okay, we'll break up into teams of two, and we'll begin with the infants and work our way up. Now let's get going."

"Hey," the woman next to Kate said. "You healthy?"

"As far as I know."

"Well, you don't have to worry about me." The woman moved her chair closer. "I'm training to be a nurse's aide. This is almost old hat to me, but you need to be certified."

"So you're a pro," Kate said.

"Not yet," she answered. "But soon. I'm Shauna, by the way."

"I'm Kate."

They stretched for a soft handshake.

AFTER seeing a brief film and observing Norman's demon-strations, each team was given an infant manikin and a foam mattress. The teams spread out on the floor and Norman waddled his rounds, making sure everyone's rescue breathing was correct.

"Jesus, this baby is filthy," Shauna said. She sprayed rubbing alcohol all over the face and wiped the rubbery skin in circular swaths. She joked, "You've got neglectful dummy parents, deadbeat dads."

"That's funny," Kate told her.

"Yeah. Okay, here I go." And Shauna started.

Watching her, Kate was glad that as babies Jeannie and Sarah had never been in such a predicament, though she panicked at those extended silences where injuries lived. Fears of crib death had floated over their naps. Jeannie always slept soundly. Sarah was colicky, her fists clenched, her toes curled, a rictus of displeasure that made Kate call the pediatrician on more than one occasion. The doctor was a patient man; Paul was not. He stayed at work till the last possible hour and often spent nights at business dinners, settling into the behavior of his own distant father. At beach parties on Long Island, children running around everywhere, babies nestled and rocked, Paul was awkward with the girls, holding them stiffly until they would invariably cry. "I'm not much good at this," he'd say, handing them off to Kate or the nurse.

Norman swayed over, his odor arriving a few seconds before his mass. Kate imagined that he was a lonely man—with some people you can simply tell that life doesn't offer the promise of companionship. She pictured him watching television with his mother, checking her pulse during the commercial breaks. "Good," he told Shauna, giving her a passing grade in the workbook.

Now it was Kate's turn. She did all of the things asked of her, and she did them well. And while there was no real drama involved, a genuine panic lit her nerves. She was being judged. Any slipups would be remembered—Shauna shaking her head, Norman slashing a red F. The whole class might notice. What neglect! How could she not know how to do this when Jeannie and Sarah were babies? If something awful had happened—God forbid—she would've been totally helpless. Even in hindsight, such ignorance is intolerable, that you can childproof outlets and stretch a fence across stairs but still not take into account the internal workings of the body, the mechanics of the heart. When Sarah was going through her drug problems, in and out of rehab for years, Paul posed an awful question to a group of friends. "Okay, here's something," he said. "Suppose your child were to die—I mean, say it's inevitable, and not from disease or illness, just an accident, a fluke—would you rather have that child die at the age of one or at the age of twenty?" Hearing this, Kate cringed and tried to change the subject, but Paul persisted. "No, I'm curious," he said.

Of course everyone knew about Sarah's difficulties.

"Well, I'll tell you," he continued. "I'd rather have the former. Saves you the anguish, the bigger loss, much more manageable that way. I know that's probably cold, but I think it's true."

Kate was outraged, not only at his bad taste, but at his ridiculous answer. Regardless of the emotional investment, she wanted to defend the joys of giving that child as much life as possible, instead of being cheap with your pain. But she remained silent.

"Yep." Paul lowered his head. "It's a pretty shitty question." Seeing him, dispirited yet proud in the candlelight, was like seeing one of those tricky perspective drawings—the vase that's also two silhouetted profiles, the young woman that's also an old woman—and while many friends stared at

Paul with contempt, Kate couldn't help but glimpse the other man poking at the margins, the man she knew so well, the man who revealed himself less and less often, but no doubt was still there.

After a few minutes of mouth-to-mouth, Norman said, "That's good." He signed his name in the workbook and moved toward the next twosome.

Shauna cheered, "Well done."

"I hate pressure."

"You were pretty cool." She looked down at the infant manikin and said, "You lucky you got mothers to take care of you."

AFTER completing Unit One, the class had a ten-minute break before tackling Unit Two: the children. Some people put on their jackets and shuffled toward the hall, their hands patting packs of cigarettes and loose change for coffee and snacks. Others retired to the safety of their belongings. Norman sat at his desk and took out a doughnut from a glaze-stained bag. Wind played the windows, and snow wisped the street below.

"No way I'm going out there," Shauna said. "I tell you, this weather turns smokers into the fools they are."

Kate told her, "My husband smokes."

"Of course he does. Hell, every man I ever been with smokes." She laughed a bit too loudly, and then said, "Been bad for my health, that's for sure."

Kate smiled.

"Sometimes, you know what, I can't believe I don't see some Surgeon General's warning stamped on their bodies, right there." She pointed to her own thigh. "The least they could do," she said.

And Kate wondered if she was on the verge of making a new friend: if the two of them would keep in touch after this class; if they would call each other on the phone and exchange daily adventures; if they would meet for lunch every week; if Shauna would come out to Long Island for weekends of tennis and golf, the members of those clubs shocked at their closeness; and if Kate would visit Shauna's apartment and worship at her church and walk around her neighborhood in a fine Sunday hat. Such a fantasy outlined itself in the ease of the conversation, as if this were the beginning of a history, the first hours of lifelong exploration. It was thrilling to Kate, like her first homosexual friend had been thrilling, an exotic shore in the distance and she was a cast-off from a land of ladies' lunches.

SOON everyone was back in the classroom, and the next section of the workbook was started, the child manikins passed out to each team. After learning what to do when a child stops breathing, they learned what to do when a child is choking. Norman demonstrated the universal distress signal, his hands grasping his throat, his mouth wide open. "When you see anyone do this," he said, "then you got to act right away with the Heimlich maneuver."

And for the next half hour the class practiced on their partners as if they were children. Kate asked Shauna, "Are you choking?" Shauna nodded. Kate told an imaginary witness to phone EMS. Shauna's eyes pleaded for help. Kate wrapped her arms around Shauna's stomach; she made a fist; she placed the fist just above the navel and well below the lower tip of the breastbone; she covered the fist with her free hand.

"Not too hard," Shauna whispered. "I had a big breakfast."

Kate answered back, "Okay," and pantomimed four abdominal thrusts.

Shauna pretended to spit out a lodged piece of candy, her tongue thwooping the phantom projectile into the middle of the room. "There it goes," she said.

"What was it?" Kate asked.

"A nasty gob-stopper. I swear those things should be forbidden to us kids."

"I guess you've learned your lesson."

"You know it, Mom." She laughed, and Kate's hands could feel each burst of welling air.

Norman swayed over. "Ticklish?" he asked.

"No, no," Shauna said. "Just cracking up."

"That can happen. Seen it before. Okay, ladies, show me how it's done."

They both took turns and proved themselves adequate, and after each team had done the same, Norman gathered everyone around and said, "Okay, I'm only going to show this to you once, so pay attention." He slid a chair in front of his stomach. "Now if you ever find yourself choking without anyone to help you, what you've got to do is find a straight-back chair and throw yourself on it so that air is forced from your abdomen. Okay. Watch carefully." Norman stepped back, his face grim. This must be the plight of the lonely, eating a meal without company, just watching TV and chewing down functional food. To Kate, it was a frightening thought, that you could die simply because nobody was left in your world to save you. Norman hurled himself onto the chair, belly-flopping on the backrest, then fell off to the side and rolled to the floor, possibly injured.

The class was shocked, and though being trained to provide emergency care, they stood there frozen.

"I'm all right," Norman groaned. "I'm all right. This always happens." He recovered his breath on all fours, a supplicant to self-preservation, and after a minute rose to his feet. He said, "My wife thinks I should quit doing this particular demonstration, that I should just explain it, but I think it's important to actually show it." He retucked his shirt, his hands disappearing into the netherworld of his pants, and Kate felt foolish at having assumed that he wasn't married and loved and happy. Norman probably came home from work and folded into the meaty arms of his wife. "Hard day," he might say, and she might answer, "Please, please, just stop with the chair, please."

AFTER Norman had fully recovered, the class learned what to do when confronted with an unconscious child with complete airway obstruction—how you thrust the abdomen with the heel of your hand in hopes of freeing the lodged object. Kate knelt over the manikin, her arms extended, her palms wet. Every time she pushed down on the gut, a leak of air came from the molded lips, a leak that defied complete airway obstruction. This mere appearance of truth would've been difficult for her daughter to handle. Complete honesty was Sarah's vanishing point, and anything false skewed the proportions. As a result, she saw the crooked world around her as a world without depth, only surface, and with every step forward she knocked into a phony backdrop. Drugs, it seems to Kate, turned her perspective into a wonderful blanket, and this blanket was warm for a while, but then it became colder outside and she needed more blankets, so she dug into the closet and pulled everything out and snuggled under a greater bulk. Once again she was warm, but she could no longer sleep or eat, she could no longer move, and that awful coldness still ate through the wool like piranha moths, and they were getting closer, ready to converge into that sad distance she had become.

This, of course, is only an assumption. Kate has never done drugs, barely even seen them except for marijuana at a few parties years ago—the joints passed around in an illicit version of afternoon tea, pinkies up with every drag and goofy talk about absolutely nothing. But that was a lower form of desperation, not her daughter's highly evolved form. For a while Kate was obsessed with why it transfixed Sarah in such a way, and she wanted to be able to understand its pull, its charm, instead of blindly denouncing it as evil. She had daydreams about knowing the lingo beyond the words, of enduring the answer in order to determine the question.

Paul, on the other hand, filed away the problems in a folder marked "Genetic Flaws," a folder that also contained his alcoholic father, his alcoholic brother, his socialist sister. "It's the crapshoot of DNA," he'd say with cold sadness. And Jeannie turned scornful. "Don't worry about me," she'd tell her mother over the phone, "wouldn't want to start a precedent, God forbid."

Kate put her finger within the manikin's mouth, sliding it along the inside of the cheek to the base of the tongue. She pretended to find something dislodged.

AFTER Unit Two, the class had another ten-minute break before finishing up with Unit Three: the adults. Once again, some people left for a brief journey outside, while others settled into their private space. Norman ate sweets pulled from a clear plastic Baggy, his fingers picking out red gummy fish and holding them aloft by their tails as if amazed by the creatures of this candy world. Shauna and Kate went down the hall toward a glowing soda machine.

"This is tiring," Kate said. "I need caffeine."

"I hear you."

Kate slipped coins into the slot, the quarters falling with clicks, and pushed the Diet Coke window—thunk!—and bent down to remove the can.

"Use the finger-sweep technique," Shauna told her.

"That's funny," Kate said.

Then Shauna asked, "Do you ever laugh, or do you just say 'That's funny' all the time?"

"Oh, I laugh. Definitely."

"Because I tell you, 'That's funny' can get on your nerves."

Kate's stomach bundled into a tight package of third-grade doubt. Maybe Shauna didn't like her, maybe she hated her, maybe she couldn't wait to get back to her friends and tell them about this humorless woman. "I'm sorry," Kate said.

Shauna reached down and grabbed her Mountain Dew. "I don't mean nothing by it. I'm just used to people actually laughing at my jokes."

"Well, you're very funny," Kate said.

"There you go again. Nothing more unfunny than to be told you're funny. Damn annoying, really." She opened the can and took a long loud sip. "Don't be upset," she said, "I'm just telling you."

Kate nodded.

"Hey, I'm just telling you, that's all. No big deal."

NORMAN said that the end was near. The human cycle had reached its culmination and now, after rescue breathing and choking, they had to learn how to save an adult from a heart attack. The manikins were claimed by a member of each team. "Here we go," Shauna said. "A real hard guy, like on *Baywatch*."

"Yes," Kate said.

His red jogging suit was in tatters, the sleeves frayed, the polyester stained, the zipper broken so that a perfectly sculpted torso was revealed with a level of immodesty popular in the 1960s. This false man was not a prime candidate for a heart attack. This was a man who cared about his body. This was a man who didn't know hope because events always turned out for the best. This was a man who swam laps in the ocean and lay on the beach without a towel. *Look at me, oh pretty girls,* this man seemed to say, as the beads of water dissolved into a briny tan. And the pretty girls, lined shoulder to shoulder, watched him, each imagining a possible match. *Look at him, just look at him, if only I could be sand.* But maybe thirty years later, this man would convert into an unhealthy, tense version of his youthful self, a man clinging to his own failed invention no matter the circumstances, a man shunning the vulnerability of anything shared. And at some point, after so much divestment, this man would sneak up into the attic and shuffle through old love letters, picking out those he once wrote in a state of exuberance, letters too embarrassing, too revealing, too weak, scrawled in a cold barracks. No, these letters had nothing to do with him now, this man would tell you without the slightest trace of contrition, and yes, these letters were balled up and thrown out with the other stuff of a finished day.

Shauna said, "You go first, honey."

"You sure?"

"I can give you tips."

"All right." Kate tied her hair with an elastic, then she shook the manikin and asked, "Are you okay?" She called out for someone to help. She checked for all she had to check. She dialed 911. She knelt next to him, the heel of her hand on his breastbone. She numbered each compression, "One and two and three . . ." until she hit fifteen. She bent over his face. She tilted his head upward. She pinched his nose and sealed her lips over his mouth. Two full breaths. She looked for his chest to rise and fall; listened and felt for escaping air; searched for a pulse. She did everything by the book, hoping it was enough to restart a life. "One and two and three. . . ." All around her she heard people counting and exhaling in a rounding rhythm. Two full breaths. She concentrated on her own work and focused on rote memory. "One and two and three. . . . " Of course nothing was happening, nothing would happen, this was make-believe, but then again, the world of melodrama did not observe the laws of cause and effect. Two full breaths. Maybe at some point a faint pulse would push against her fingers, and this young man would stir, and he would smile. "One and two and three. . . ."And he would tell her all those near-death clichés, the white light, the tunnel, and she would pretend that they were new and wonderful, like a husband and wife walking down the beach, the surf crashing, the water a silver-white mercury, the sun dipping into the horizon, the sky showing them, just briefly, what was hidden inside clouds. Two full breaths.

At the Déjà Vu

I WENT TO Mississippi to kill a turkey, it being April and the time to kill turkeys. Not that I'm much of a hunter, just a dabbler in such manly pursuits. Once or twice a year I go to a sporting reserve in upstate New York and shoot pen-raised birds, pheasant and chucker mostly. These birds are set out in the morning, hidden within the brush like Easter eggs for bloodthirsty children. Hours later you walk through fields with a guide, a few springer spaniels up ahead sniffing and pissing and squirting a constant skid of diarrhea. The guide tells you, "I think they're on to something," pretending that a wildness is involved instead of a hand-placed precision. Soon the dogs freeze, tails stiff, paws lifted and limp—no matter the circumstances, a beautiful thing to behold. The guide whispers, "Okay, okay, okay," and arranges you for a clear shot. The overall scene is briefly spoiled when he's forced to flush the tame birds by kicking and yelling at them, but when you put the gun to your shoulder and pull the trigger and see the immediate effect—a pheasant freezes, then tumbles to the ground—well, it is satisfying.

So I packed a duffel bag for the trip south, breaking down my .12-gauge shotgun and slipping the separate bits into old athletic socks, like some sort of assassin on a secret mission. I surrounded these cotton-encased sausages with innocuous polo shirts and khaki pants, the condiments of a law-abiding citizen. Gretchen, my wife of two years, my second in six years, watched me as I did this.

"You're so serious," she said.

"How's that?"

"Your face, it's like this is a science." She sat at the end of the bed, her face far from scientific though she benefited from a certain pharmaceutical science. You really noticed it in her eyes. They wanted to be nervous, constantly scanning details and questioning their particular relevance, but something in the pills held them from panic, kept them steady like hands restraining a small wild animal.

I said to her, "Well, it's illegal. You know what happens if I get busted with this thing in an airport?"

"No."

"It's a twenty-five-thousand-dollar fine and a few months in jail. Or something like that."

"Really?"

"Yes." Then I realized that this information might strain the limits of her medication, so I added, "But no one ever gets caught. Never. Not if you're careful."

"Oh."

"So don't worry."

"Okay." She picked up two pairs of socks, each tightly balled within itself. She weighed them with utmost concentration, her upper lip curled and tucked over her lower teeth, an expression I recognized from her tennis-playing days. She used to have a very nasty spin serve, a left-handed slice, and on ad points she would force you into the fence. But this was when her killer instinct was aimed at others. She made a few juggling pantomimes, trying to figure out the basic mechanics between object and air and self. I went to the bureau and grabbed some other socks.

"You sure you're going to be all right for the weekend?" I asked.

"What?"

"This weekend, are you going to be all right?"

"Oh, I've got things to do."

"Good. The plantation number is by the phone, just in case." I zipped up the duffel, feeling like a surgeon when he turns a wound into a scar, then leaves the recovering patient behind. "Well, I'm off," I said.

"You sure are."

You shoot turkeys on the ground, in the head, as they strut in front of a replica of a hen, the hot blood of desire shading their necks purple, drowning out all reason for the hope of a thrill. Sitting in the airport bar, my flight to Atlanta an hour from boarding, a brief vision of blow-up sex toys played in my head, of lonely men, young and old, seeing a group of helpless naked women lounging by the highway, their mouths finishing the perfect O of hello, their breasts better than saline implants, their vaginas shaved. Of course these men would lock up their brakes and sprint for introductions, no matter if married or not. And they'd never notice the lack of movement in the bodies or the ridge where the two plastic halves collide. They'd probably be shot in the head as well. The clean kill of the lusty stupid.

I ordered another drink, rationalizing a double whiskey with a general fear of flying, not my fear, but the fear of the people around me. Anxiety lit their faces with an ashen neon glow, the noble gas flickering thoughts of *We might die.* They treated the booths like the trenches of Verdun, and I was almost ready for a rendition of "La Marseillaise" before a charge toward the gate. Maybe I'd sing "Wacht am Rhein" as historical counterpoint.

I rechecked my plane tickets: New York to Atlanta; Atlanta to Jackson, Mississippi. During the layover I'd meet Wilson Plagett, my host for the weekend, a college friend whose uncle owned a plantation teeming with wild turkeys.

I had convinced Wilson that a little hunting would do us both some good. "Blast the hell out of something," I told him on the phone.

"You think?" he said.

"Why not? I mean, why not?"

Wilson said, "Okay," his response so quick and casual that it briefly deflated my excitement and left me feeling small with my idea of fun.

Over a loudspeaker a female voice announced the pre-boarding of my flight, for the clumsy young and the senior frail and the privileged few. Some people reluctantly rose, strapping on their gear and tamping out their cigarettes, finishing their drinks. The first wave. I waited for the third wave of final boarding.

I WAS sitting in the way back of the airplane, in the seats that can't recline, across from the bank of narrow bathroom stalls, a sweet odor of antiseptic blue water wafting out with each entry and exit. A very bad situation. Now add babies. A slew of them surrounded me, all newborns, wrapped so that they resembled linen props in a Broadway play. Their crying was incredible. I could hear them in first class, but from that distance and in that atmosphere of civilized travel, I mistook them for some sort of pneumatic device employed to restock the galley. As I got closer, I recognized the baldly human quality in the noise. I trudged forward, my boarding pass held out in front of me, and I stared at its high number like a gambler who knows his horse is a loser after the first furlong. I said, "Shit," just above a whisper, envying those in front of me who broke left or right, cashing out, while I continued forward, busted. 46C. I stopped. The eight women who held the eight babies smiled at me.

I found the nearest flight attendant and pleaded, "I can't sit back there, I mean, no way, it's a nightmare, almost a bad joke, ha ha ha, but really I just can't."

"I'm sorry, sir, but it's a full flight." She was an older flight attendant, in her youth probably a stewardess, and she carried the washed-out, overly made-up, seen-everything sheen of a service-industry veteran. These are women you don't fuck with. Their dreams of being whisked off by executives have been dashed years ago, and their routes are no longer European hot spots but East Coast hubs, and now they must wait on inelegant passengers while they yearn for a minor disaster to break the boredom of the day.

I asked, "Is there anything in first class?"

"No. This is a full flight."

"Please. Anything."

"Sir, you're going to have to sit down. We're in our cross-check."

"Well I'm in the goddamn penalty box."

She almost grabbed me by the lapels in a shakedown of what's what. "Listen. If you don't want your seat, we have plenty of standbys who'd kill to get on this flight. Okay?"

Heads on either side upturned as if a bride and groom were having a spat at the altar. Their discomfort subdued me. "I'm sorry," I said.

"That's all right. Just sit down."

"I will."

"Good."

"But I want to put in my order early for some whiskey. That's the least you can do."

And she smiled and showed me her wrinkles, along her eyes and mouth, and I knew I was with someone who understood desperation. "I will make your flight as comfortable as possible."

"Thank you," I said.

Back at row 46 the baby-holding women still smiled, and I settled into the colic and tried to meditate, to breathe in and out, to find transcendence in a hum, a loving mantra. No dice. So I took refuge in earthly distractions. I glanced at the emergency pamphlet—the cartoon people with impossible cartoon composure—then at the in-flight magazine with its inane articles on travel—"St. Louis: Gateway to Dreams"—and then at the book I had lugged with me, a history of warfare aptly titled *A History of Warfare*. For the last month I'd been stuck on the Battle of Actium, the bookmark a flag of surrender. When the plane started to lumber down the runway, I stopped reading and began concentrating on aerodynamics, on airfoil and the physical certainty of lift and drag, a principle of science, no less, a goddamn rule, a fucking law! Even the babies briefly quieted with profound recognition. Together, we waited for these precepts to kick in, and of course they did, and soon we were above New York, banking over Queens, climbing past New Jersey and leveling off under God knows where. The "Fasten Seat Belt" symbol dinged dim. A few people immediately rose to their feet as if freed from the chains of enslavement. And eventually the flight attendant dumped six tiny bottles of Jack Daniels on my lap. "Now be good," she told me. I nodded, a five-year-old with his new blocks, and I proceeded to build a castle on my tray table, a feudal estate with turrets, and like Alice, I grew smaller as I drank, but in the end there wasn't enough booze to make me a lord of anything.

WHEN the plane touched in Atlanta and pulled into the gate, and the aisle filled with people, I stayed in my seat, happy to be last, a position I've cherished since high school. Not much of a limerick, no rhymes, no bawdiness, but a lack of effort is the best revenge against forced meter. Once everyone had deplaned, movement came over me. I said good-bye to the flight crew who stood by the cockpit in a thanks-for-flying tableau. "Nice landing," I said to the pilot as if I were Chuck Yeager. And after the solitary walk through the jetway, the colon of transportation, I was flushed into the swirl of the terminal, not the usual combination of activity and

passivity, but something different, something blunt and jar-
ring and frightening—sobs of joy, from men and women
cradling babies, my babies, in their arms. A banner spelled
WELCOME. Balloons were tethered to anything that could
take a knot, though some had escaped and were sadly stuck
to the ceiling.

"Hey, Tom." Wilson Plagett patted me on the back. "I
thought maybe you missed your flight."

"Nope. I was in the tail with the screaming babies."

"Ouch," Wilson said, his well-managed face smiling. I'd
last seen him at our tenth reunion, where I found myself
naked in a lake at three in the morning, trying to convince
everyone else to *just loosen up*. Wilson was the only one
who joined me, a new party compatriot, having held off at
college for the sake of a future public life that never panned
out. Instead of governor, he was now an insurance executive
who played a ton of business golf. "Some guy told me," he
said, "that these are orphans from China. All girls. They do
awful things to girls over there."

"China's a cruel place."

"I've heard that. Anyway, these folks are adopting
them."

"Brave."

"Sure is. I couldn't do it." Wilson checked his watch, a
huge Rolex that could sink a drowning man. "We've got
time to kill. A drink, maybe?"

"If you insist."

NOW I'M not Southern, but when I'm around Southerners
or down South or just plain drunk, this weird accent inflects
my speech, and I become broad and expansive, convinced
that this is the most natural thing in the world, almost
authentic, though I've been told I sound more like Big
Daddy as played by Dustin Hoffman. So by the time Wilson
and I landed in Mississippi and rented a car for the two-hour

drive and took advantage of the wonderful convenience of a drive-thru liquor store, I was feeling good and Southern, eating a stick of beef jerky and wondering why I didn't eat a stick every day.

"Fucking good," I said while chewing.

"What?"

"This."

"Stuff'll kill you." Wilson's eyes were intent on the road. It was late dusk, a difficult light that turned passing shadows into phantom dogs who jumped out in front of the car. Wilson was quick on the brake, his body hunched over the wheel, and in my inflated state of Southern charm, I began recollecting past drunken behavior.

"Did I ever tell you about my crazed trip to the Bahamas with some woman I met at a bar? No?" So I told him. It happened almost three years ago, during a cold New York winter, when I was married to the other woman, a high school sweetheart, and I went out for a drink after a half-day of work, a few friends joining me, and soon those drinks compiled like a late payment on a loan, and we found ourselves at another bar, and another bar, running from debt until I met this woman. She was quite beautiful, her nose sharp with cartilage which created a ridge. This one physiological feature seemed to define her face, like a hilltop cathedral in a small European village, the outlying lips and eyes and cheekbones and chin modeled with a similar devotion. Think of Chartres with breasts, a mysterious presence imbued with a conflicted history of worship. But I was drunk at the time.

We started talking about the weather and tennis—she was an ardent player—and how this weather made tennis impossible, which was too bad because she could kick my ass. I didn't doubt it. She let me feel the muscle in her left forearm. Quite impressive. And when she moved, little air was displaced, as if she were designed for speed. The afternoon turned to tequila shots—she insisted—and warmer weather entered our discussion, of tropics, of beaches, of sun-baked clay courts, and we began leaning into each other until we had leaned into a taxi and leaned into an airport and leaned into a flight to Great Abaco Island, an awful place in the Bahamas, where we continued the night, drinking frothy fruity drinks and hitching in a cheap motel, the next day buying tacky clothes, playing absurd tennis, napping but never really sleeping. The hangover was all-encompassing, the physical spilling into the psychological so that you questioned your life and your decisions and your behavior. To avoid such thoughts, and to cool down and feel weightless, I went snorkeling on my own, leaving Gretchen—yes, Gretchen—to recover in the shade. As I swam out into the cay, I saw no signs of aquatic life, no coral, no fish, only sand and murky water. My stomach started to unsettle, and my mouth filled with acidy saliva, and within seconds I was retching into my snorkel, shooting out a stream of vomit like some bowery whale. It was a very low moment, throwing up into the ocean, until these fish, I think they were parrot fish, with small puckered mouths, suddenly appeared and proceeded to eat the lowly species of my puke.

"That's disgusting," Wilson said.

"No. It was spectacular," I said. "All this color, a swarm of it, just colorful, the fish, I mean."

"Still disgusting."

"They were hungry."

"Uh, please." Wilson squirmed, then asked, "That's how you met Gretchen?"

"Basically. At least a version of her."

"That's how the whole thing started?"

"Yep."

"That's quite a story."

"One of many. But the only one with fish involved." I reached into the backseat and dug my hand into the booze-filled bag—the housewarming present—my face lit with the glow of what was once wild experience.

A HALF hour later we turned off the highway and drove past towns instead of exit signs. The darkness held squalor, you could just sense it as you can sense rain on a clear day. Roadside buildings were put up with house-of-card construction, the light within revealing cracks. The live oaks that seemed to twist in pain like Dante's suicide woods, the dripping Spanish moss the drool of indulgent last words, and once making this connection, easy lugubriousness took over and tinted the odor of dank soil and perfumed plants— azaleas, magnolias, camellias—into an open-coffin wake, and the distant sounds of swampy nature into an unknown beast half-submerged.

"How much further?" I asked.

"Forty-five minutes."

"I need to get some food in me."

Wilson was interested in making good time, so he feigned deafness. But I pressed further. "Maybe we could stop somewhere."

"Uhm . . ."

"Get a burger or something. A drink."

"Another drink?"

"Why not? I mean, are they expecting us at the house?"

"Yes and no."

"Is there a big dinner planned tonight?"

"No."

"What's our commitment?"

"Well, hunting in the morning. Early morning. Pre-dawn."

"That gives us about eight hours to grab a bite."

"Well." Wilson rocked his head with internal debate, then smiled like the lame duck he was and said, "We can stop in Kosciusko."

Some people don't know fun until it's their last option.

• • •

THERE ARE secrets to turkey hunting. Calling is very important. The merely adequate are able to mimic a hen by
scratching a piece of cedar on slate, while the truly adept use
a diaphragm call, a small whistle tucked in the mouth, so
that their hands can be free to aim and kill. *Yelp-yelp-yelp* is
the sound you're trying to capture; *yelp-yelp-yelp* will bring
you a mate. But that's only half the game. Stillness and cam-
ouflage are also essential, not moving as you rest against a
tree and pretend to be an innocent swath of moss holding a
.12-gauge shotgun.

Walking into Mervin's Shack in downtown Kosciusko, I
possessed none of these qualities. I was still wearing my suit
from work, and even though the jacket and tie were off, and
the sleeves of my shirt were rolled up, the people inside
turned and watched me enter. All talk briefly hushed so that
sizzling meat became the primary conversation. Wilson
guided me to a free table, the flotsam of spilt ketchup and
french fries on its orange surface. A waiter came over and
wiped away the mess and deposited two menus. He had the
loose face of a stroke victim.

"Howdy," I said, sometimes getting confused with the
West and the South, between twang and drawl, talking like
an Oklahoman.

"Hey."

"Can we get two beers?"

"BYOB," he said.

"Huh?"

Wilson translated, "It's bring you're own," then he said
to the waiter, "We'll take two Cokes on ice."

"No booze?" I asked Wilson.

"Guess not."

"Should I go back to the car?"

"Don't bother."

A man at the counter glanced over, his eyes scrutinizing

us as if we were soaked in gasoline. He slipped off the stool
and made his way to our table, his left leg kicking a large
cooler. "Hey," he said.

"Hey."

"You boys with the FBI?"

"I'm not," I said. "But I'm not too sure about him."

He smiled. There was gold in his teeth. He opened up the
cooler and revealed the lovely brown necks of submerged bottles. "I brought you your beer," he said. "Knew you'd forget."

"You're a friend," I answered, enjoying this black-
market code. Wilson was less at ease, his knee nervous under
the table.

The man set down two bottles. "Oh," he said, "Did you
remember to bring that money I lent you?"

"Sure did." I handed him a twenty.

"Can't make change," he said.

"We'll take it in kind."

When the racketeer left, we had eight bottles on the table,
and Wilson was already pleased with the adventure, his ner-
vousness turned into giddiness, and he probably could've
stopped right there and weaved a story for friends back
home, of eating chicken with gravy and mashed potatoes
and drinking illegal beer.

BEFORE leaving, I called Gretchen from the back of
Mervin's Shack, at a pay phone surrounded by industrial
jars of mayonnaise. The answering machine picked up but I
knew enough to disregard that as any sign of vacancy. After
the beep, I said, "Hey Gretch, it's me. Are you home? Hello
hello hello."

There was a click, and a fumble, and a curse, then she
answered. "It's you."

"Just wanted to tell you I made it here all right."

"You sure did."

"Met Wilson, no problem. Flight was easy."

"Good," she said.

"You know, I was thinking," I began telling her, "that I don't think I've been away from you for the last nine months. Not one night. Not one single night. Nope."

"You don't have to call."

"I want to. Thought maybe you tried the plantation and I wasn't there and that might've—" My hip edged a mayonnaise jar from the pile; it fell to the floor but luckily it was plastic and all it did was sway in a mesmerizing half-circle. "Just calling to say hi."

"Where are you?" Her voice had lost the ability to clothe a question properly; instead, she spoke with the threadbare tone of a bureaucrat.

"I'm at some restaurant in a town I can't pronounce," I said.

"Oh. You been drinking?"

"A little. Well, a lot. What have you been doing?"

"Killed a turkey yet?"

"No. That's tomorrow. What did you have for dinner?"

"Warm there?"

"Yeah. Everything all right?"

She took a deep breath, though it was far from a sigh, more of a public access of air. "Do you want me to say no?"

"What?"

"Just curious. Strap on the old Superman outfit and fly back, maybe?"

"Come on, Gretch," I said.

"I'm all right," she said.

"Huh?"

"I'm all right, that's all. Truly."

"Great." I looked over toward Wilson, sitting alone, uncomfortable in such a place, his eyes concentrating on a beer bottle, his fingers picking at the label. "I better get going," I told her. "Just wanted to touch base and say I made it here in one piece."

"You sure did."

• • •

OUTSIDE, the streets of Kosciusko were busy with cars cruising the strip of Main Street, making constant circles from one end to the other, like animals too long contained in a cage and now left to pace the edges of their existence. "We should probably get to the plantation now," Wilson said.

"Still early," I said.

"Not really. Not anymore. Long day tomorrow."

"Come on, a couple more drinks. Let's have some fun, Mr. Governor. The campaign's over and we lost."

Wilson smiled. "I don't know if I can keep up," he said.

"Sure you can."

"I don't know if I want to."

"Sure you do."

I started walking ahead, happy to take charge in such circumstances, a man with an understanding of what to do and where to go, a man with contingencies, a man more interested in the military than the political. Nights of depravity made for mornings of pain which led to days of grace. A syllogism for drunken behavior. Wilson soon followed.

OFTENTIMES, when turkey hunting, you'll sit for hours against a tree, calling and calling; listening; calling and calling, yet nothing will answer, nothing will happen, nothing will emerge in that early morning to awaken you. These are smart birds, though most people know them as domesticated livestock waiting for the November hatchet of a mass sacrifice, so stupid that they can drown in a rainstorm, so ridiculous that their name has become a put-down. Gretchen cooked turkey only once, and that was last July in the midst of a heat wave. She sporadically tested herself as a homemaker—knitting, gardening, interior design—each foray lasting only long enough to prove that she was capable of the task. This led to a complicated sweater with missing arms, a garden halfway planted in colorful annuals, a chintzy living room that didn't match any other room in the house, and a perfectly prepared turkey served with potato chips and raw, uncut carrots.

Wilson asked, "Did you talk to Gretchen?" We were heading down Main Street, in search of a proper bar to have a proper drink.

"Yep."

"How is she?"

"Off and on. Mostly on, nowadays."

"That's good."

"Sure."

To our left, in a small gated park, we passed a grass mound, bulged as if an elephant had been buried beneath. A plaque informed us that this was a tribute to Tadeusz Kościuszko, a Polish patriot who fought on the side of the American Revolutionary Army in the War of Independence. He was a hero in many a campaign, and in 1934 the town of Perish was renamed in his honor. Three thousand school-children contributed cupfuls of earth from their yards to build this monument.

I said to Wilson, "Have you ever heard of him?"

"Nope. I thought it was some local tribe." Wilson was a buff of the War of 1812, feeling that the Revolutionary War and the Civil War were already overfilled with buffs. He loved to discuss the Battle of New Orleans and the consequences of poor communication. I was still stuck on the Battle of Actium, where Cleopatra abandoned Mark Antony in the face of defeat.

"I like Perish better," I said. "Easier to pronounce at least. Perish. I live in Perish. I'm Perishian."

"Yeah, whatever."

Down the street we came across a place with a glowing sign scripted in the window: The Déjà Vu. I peered inside, my hands shading the streetlight glare. I saw people milling along the feedline of the bar; I heard jukebox music playing Motown; I felt social vibrations reverberating against the glass; I asked, "How about here?" in a fog of moist breath.

"Here?"

"Yeah."

"You think?"

"Why not?"

"One drink," Wilson said.

And I said, "Let's just play it by ear."

We pushed through the door. The atmosphere cooled as if we had brought in a draft and sucked out warm comfortable air, the two of us an arctic front that swept toward cracked leather stools. The bartender, a chubby man wearing a Key West T-shirt, paced back and forth in the trough behind the bar, popping off tops of beer bottles with a powerful flick of his wrist. He had the avuncular appearance of a fishing guide. He asked us, "What can I get you?"

"A beer," Wilson said.

The bartender nodded, then he turned to me. I pointed to a juice dispenser positioned behind the bar. Liquid cascaded down the clear plastic shell like turquoise rain on a window. "What's that?" I asked.

"We call it a hand grenade," he said. "Knock your socks off."

"Yeah?"

"You want?"

"Two."

"I'm all set," Wilson said.

"No no no no," I told him. "We have to soak up the local flavor. That's part of the experience."

The bartender ended up listening to me, the machine humming when it poured. "Six bucks," he said. I paid with a twenty and left a four-dollar tip. My wallet was bursting with twenties. Whenever traveling, I always overestimate my expenses. Wilson nervously noticed the wad.

"So cheap," I said.

"You better be careful with so much cash," he said.

"That's racist," I said.

"What?"

"If we were in some fancy place you wouldn't think that."

"Jesus, that's an asshole thing to say."

"I'm sorry." I lifted up the glass. "Cheers," I said.

"Yeah."

I tossed the hand grenade down my throat. Wilson sipped. It was sweet, a combination of lemonade and grape juice mixed with the unmistakable numbing of grain alcohol. After the first taste everything else dwelled in the aftertaste. "Whoa," I said.

Wilson pushed the glass away. "I can't drink this."

"Sure you can."

"No. I don't want to drink it. I think we should go," he said.

"Don't be a pussy."

"I'm leaving."

"No, you're not."

"My uncle's probably worried."

I touched him on the shoulder. "Wilson, you're a thirty-two-year-old man."

"Exactly why I'm going." He slid off the stool. "You coming?"

"No. I'm staying. I'll meet you there. Cheeawah Plantation, right?"

"That's insane. We're hunting in the morning, remember? It was your fucking idea."

"But this is fun."

"How you going to get there?"

"I'll hitchhike."

The conversation continued, trapped in a long rally, until I put the point away with an overhead slam of rudeness—"You're still that fucking college loser nobody liked!"—and

Wilson flashed anger and left the bar. Game over. I thought for a moment that he was going to hit me, really pummel me, but he just reeled and walked away.

TURKEYS are prized for particular characteristics. A great ruffled tail. Sharp spurs on the legs. Those items are often cut from the bird and kept as keepsakes to the hunt, the tail fanned on a wall, the spurs hanging from a rearview mirror. The more dedicated will actually stuff the bird so that the long beard can be remembered, and the puffed body, bronzed and iridescent, can be preserved in its last living pose. Others will ask the taxidermist to mount the bird in flight, so that the mighty wingspan is spread and any indication of death is left behind on the ground.

At the Déjà Vu, a large clock, the type often seen in classrooms, filled in the seconds between minutes, a full circle that somehow encompassed the sun and the planets and the laws of brilliant men passed down to ignorant me, sitting in this bar, drinking hand grenades, pretending that this repetition of time was gentle when in reality it was painfully linear.

"Daylight Saving's tomorrow," the bartender said.

"Yeah?"

"That's right. Tomorrow night you lose an hour to drink."

"How's that go again?"

He smiled and said, "Spring forward, fall backward, that's the easy way to remember it."

"That's right. Always forget."

The overhead lights were on, so bright now, and most of the people had cleared out for a party somewhere. Glasses were being collected. A young man was mopping down the floor and throwing bottles into a large trash bin, an awful noise.

"So tomorrow," the bartender told me, "you'll have to

start happy hour an hour earlier in order to offset the government watches."

"Yeah?"

"Yep."

"But I have to go now?"

"Sorry to say. You're a good tipper."

"Any cabs in this town?" I asked.

"Here? No."

"Can you give me a ride?"

"Me? Sorry, no."

I got up and felt all too clearheaded, as if I had been drinking to stay sober. "Good-bye now," I said, a bit disappointed that I hadn't made friends, that I hadn't stumbled onto a group of others who were off to do wicked things—to steal road signs or wake up single women with pebble-throwing entreaties. Instead, I just sat alone at the bar, the stools on either side of me empty. No one even tried to pick a fight.

In the warm after hours, I walked aimlessly down the street, my thumb stuck out for nothing. I glanced around like someone traveling by himself, someone who wants to see glorious sights yet doesn't want to see them alone, someone looking sideways for a friend. And I thought about giving Gretchen a call and telling her that I was alone in this town and wished that she was with me, at my side, the two of us tipsy or maybe just flat-out wasted. But I didn't spot any pay phones.

Up ahead, the lush grass of Kosciuszko Mound was too inviting to pass up a roost. I lay down at the crest. Live oaks, their trunks in deep shadows, twisted so that sky was glimpsed through crooks and curves, the Spanish moss hanging luminescent, as if a distant relative to the moon. And before passing out, I imagined children, practically babies, little girls rescued from a cruel fate who come to this place and dump cupfuls of earth from old Perish to a new beginning, slowly covering me in the dank soil, legs disappearing, torso disappearing, arms disappearing, now just a head remains, the final reminder, but soon that will be gone too and only a monument will live on.

MAY I ask, has this ever happened to you?

Still in Motion

A SINGLE REFERENCE brought them here:

He said he would not ransom Mortimer; forbade my
tongue to speak of Mortimer; but I will find him when
he lies asleep, and in his ear I'll holla 'Mortimer!'
Nay, I'll have a starling shall be taught to speak nothing but 'Mortimer,' and give it to him to keep his
anger still in motion.

There it is, the one and only starling in the entire works
of Shakespeare, the verse, like the bird, more menacing than
beautiful. But in 1890 the Society Friends of New York
(picture a group of bored Victorian matriarchs escorted by
one lonely Columbia professor of English) decided that the
full range of the Bard's winged creatures should be repre-
sented here in America, for culture's sake, for heaven's sake.
So with little fanfare, they released sixty starlings into the
Ramble of Central Park. The next year, for good measure,
they released forty more. A hundred birds and a hundred
years later, the country seems to speak nothing but Mortimer.

And recently, Debbie Reynolds (her unfortunate married
name, a name she came this close to not taking, but certainly

better than Slotnick) has fallen into the habit of sitting on her porch, a Ruger 10/22 rifle with a Ram-Line 30-round banana clip slung across her lap, ready to shoot the storming marauders. She overlooks the elaborate purple-martin houses, two of them with eighteen apartments apiece, and waits for the Luftwaffe to strike. Starlings really are the Nazis of the bird world, their sleek plumage SS black leather, their song Nuremberg cheers, their attitude all blitzkrieg. They land on the perches and poke their beaks inside with Gestapo-like tactics—*tseeeer, tseeer*—then seize the nests of the defenseless and fling out the flightless chicks with irrepressible zeal—*whooee, whooee.* But before they can turn the backyard into Poland, Debbie takes aim and picks them off with considerable skill, usually getting three before the rest fly away. Her personal best is six, though with a proper silencer she could vastly improve her kill ratio. *Thwump! Thwump! Thwump!*

"A silencer!" her husband says, a bit shocked at this news. "They're totally illegal."

"Oh, come on, take it easy. I'm half kidding." Debbie smiles with half-seriousness, her hands skillfully breaking down the gun for careful cleaning, the parts spread across the kitchen table.

"Jesus, I married a hitman," Chester jokes, hoping for some levity in the situation, though her behavior has started to concern him. Just the other weekend Debbie ran naked from the shower and stormed out onto the porch with the 10/22. "I heard something," she muttered, her eyes searching the sky for intruders. But there was no confrontation, no starlings, so she shot a poaching squirrel instead. "I love my new scope," she said.

And Chester told her to get inside.

"Relax. No one can see me."

"You're turning into a hillbilly," he said.

"Oh, shut up." A puddle was forming at her feet, darkening the wood, and the morning light seemed to favor her wet body as if the sun hungered for an opportunity to melt flesh. "We're in the boonies anyway," she said.

"This is hardly the boonies."

"Oh, please, this is the WASP version of the Ozarks." Debbie reached down and picked up the expelled shell casing and sniffed the residual cordite, a heady odor. "Blue trash," she said. "The Hatfields and the McCoys by way of Ralph Lauren."

"Yeah, whatever."

"Moonshine and Chardonnay."

"Okay, funny enough. Now please just get dressed," he said.

"Yes, sir." And she marched back inside, the 10/22 on her shoulder.

Chester sat down on the rocking chair and gazed out at the rented view: ten acres abutted by woods. The two of them moved to Millbrook about ten months ago. Chester wanted to leave the city, wanted fresh air and grass, wanted to work at home, wanted to shuck complexity in favor of simplicity, wanted to start a family, wanted a basic happiness that he couldn't find in New York. And Debbie had been mugged at knifepoint. She was walking down First Avenue after a late dinner with girlfriends and up ahead she noticed a black man coming toward her. She made a point of not crossing the street, of not clutching her purse, of not falling into the bilateral world of racial stereotypes; in fact, she imagined a pleasant smile on her face and hoped that this thought would somehow reflect positively on her features, a benign faith against unwarranted fear. And as she was pushed against a storefront grate, a distance settled on her, about a ten-foot perspective, which made everything in her life remote. That's me? And she couldn't believe it. That's really me? Right there? With a knife under my throat? Debbie Reynolds in peril? And this distance seemed to stay with her as if, on that night, time was cut into the before and after of an indifferent history.

CHESTER leans across the table and scoops up a few loose .22 cartridges. They almost feel pleasant in his hand, cool to the touch, so smooth, the brass casings clinking together like high-powered worry beads. He holds one between his thumb and index finger, all of this velocity briefly restrained, but tomorrow, or the next day, the bullet will be ripping toward a starling's breast. While mowing the lawn, he'll often come across a fallen bird, the wings frozen in their final frantic strokes, the tips sticking up in the grass with lonely surrender, and suddenly he's the choreman of the killing fields.

"Hey, Angel of Death," he says to Debbie.

Debbie stops oiling the magazine assembly and pre-tends—"Ha ha ha"—to laugh.

Chester tells her that he has a surprise.

"And what would that be?" she asks.

"A trip," he says, "kind of a seventh-anniversary trip. Just get away for a while, you know, have an adventure."

"An adventure?"

"Yeah. And maybe it'll help us with this whole preg-nancy deal. Relax us a bit."

Debbie frowns. For the last three months they've been try-ing to start a family, trying to catch up with their friends: the friends with the two kids, the three kids, the one kid in college and the one kid in diapers, the stepkids and half-kids, the adopted Chinese kid, the autistic kid with absolutely no idiot savantness, all those kids, the cute kids and the ugly kids, that are dragged along wherever the parents go, the kid foodstuff and shitstuff jammed in vinyl bags, the kid seats buckled in the backseats of cars, the kid toys lost and must be found, the kid strollers parked with the littlemost care for shins, the kid hands empty and forever needy. Chester and

Debbie, the friends always ask, why don't you guys have kids?

"We've only just begun." And Debbie immediately regrets the Karen Carpenter allusion. "It takes a while," she says.

"Oh, I know, I know. But I've kind of planned this trip, heard about it on TV, on some travel program about great escapes, and I thought it would be a nice change of pace." Chester pauses, hoping that he won't have to bring up the last defense of nonrefundable tickets. "The Galápagos," he says.

"The Galápagos?"

"Yeah, a cruise around the islands."

"Jesus."

"It'll be fun." Chester grins, the cartridge still pinched between his fingers, a symbol he projects into words. "The birthplace of evolution," he says.

"Of Darwinism," she corrects. "Evolution has no birth. I think that's the point of it."

But Chester isn't listening. He's dreamily watching the bullet float through space while Debbie strains for the background chatter of attack.

THERE are no starlings on the Galápagos Islands. Feral pigs, yes. Domesticated goats, sure. Dogs and cats, certainly. But no starlings. They don't belong here, not like the finches and the mockingbirds and the boobies (blue-footed and white-footed) and the albatrosses and the frigate birds and, of course, the tourists. Debbie finds herself watching these people more than the animals. She's embarrassed to be classified in the same category. Bullshit about Americans being the worst, the Germans are much more repulsive. They condescend to the animals, mock them by huddling and whispering, gloating at how easy it would be to conquer this place. And the dumb-ass Australians pretend to wrestle with the bull sea lions, the beachmasters with their harems. *Hoy!* The pasty British grin imperiously at the mere mention of Darwin, common nationality their last brag. The French are always checking the time for unknown reasons. Canadians, no matter how intelligent, sound witless with that vowelly accent. And the Dutch are too thin.

On the beach, everyone is snapping pictures with equal frenzy—*ca-click, ca-click, ca-click*—while the animals laze around as if this were Cannes and all the paparazzi gadflies and tickbirds, the price to be paid for environmental fame. The sea lions are the flavor of the moment, the beach covered with them and the waves washing in more. An American family of five seems tempted to dress up one of the critters with a hat and sunglasses—something they probably do to their dog back home—but the naturalists, a constant swarm of khaki, have a mantra of limited human contact. There's no ingrained fear of man, no mistrust, no hostility, so please don't touch the animals, don't feed them, don't do anything that might spoil this Eden on earth. How would you like uninvited strangers making a mess of your living room? So be respectful. But people can't help laughing at the exposed sexual equipment of the beachmasters. They're hung like horses!

Chester, a video camera strapped to his hand, stands a few yards from his wife and gently prods the air in front of him. "Why don't you get a little closer to the animals? You know, maybe bend down next to one. It'll look great."

"Who are you? Marion Perkins?"

"Who?"

"Never mind."

"Well, you have to do something."

"No," she says. "Too touristy."

"Too touristy."

"Yeah."

"Well . . ." But Chester holds off from the possible rant: Too touristy! What the hell do you expect! It's the fucking

Galápagos Islands, a tourist's mecca, a Disney World of the natural world. Now get over there so I can capture the moving quality of this place. But instead, he tries a different approach. "How about you filming me?"

"I'm too tired."

"Too tired?"

"Yeah. And it's hot."

"C'mon."

"No. I'm serious."

Debbie pulls out a cigarette from her fanny pack and lights up. "How's this for action?"

"I wish you wouldn't smoke."

"I'm not pregnant yet."

"Well, you might be."

"I'm not. Trust me."

This stubbornness, bitterness, viciousness, Chester was hoping that the trip might reintroduce Debbie to a more relaxed state. Maybe it's because she's off the pill, her body reacquainting itself with fertility, with more painful cramps, with more massive bleeding, with more tampons a day, with more haphazard a system. No more daily doses of progesterone, squeezed from the corpus luteum of pregnant sows, synthesized in a lab, packaged in a plant, prescribed by an OB-GYN, sold by a pharmacist, and punched out of a daisy-wheel calendar. So neat and tidy—your own moon held in a cheap plastic shell. Who knows? Maybe a chemical imbalance is the root to her bitchiness.

Chester goes over and wraps a beefy arm around Debbie, squeezing her shoulder, but she brushes him away like a molesting stepfather. Stop it! All this performing. A perfunctory exhibition of togetherness. It's the same with their sex life right now; it's not about them anymore, it's about an other, a hopeful zygote that directs their lovemaking with imperious Catholic precision. The two of them are missionaries of the missionary, every night of estrus considered a holy communion, a transubstantiation into flesh. Chester climbs on top of Debbie and holds her head in his intertwined fingers; he kisses her gently; he doe-eyes her until she almost pukes. And then he begins not to screw, lay, ball, frig, or fuck, but to make a baby, create a life, genesis, his ass pumping with extra vigor, pepping up Team Milt for the big meet. Oh, the beauty! This is why we're here on this planet! Debbie hears this and she wants to disappear into the comforter. Why continue the breed, with its inevitable genetic flaws, its damaged psyche, its mortal terror and suffering? Why not simply stop? All that is beautiful eventually turns nasty anyway, so why pretend otherwise? And aren't we evolved enough not to fall into the same overpopulated trap? Let the others do it: the trailer-park girls, the religious, the disenfranchised, the Third Worlders, the egotists with their family names, the hopeless striving for pampered hope. So every night for the last month Debbie has slipped in her old diaphragm—she's had it since college—and she's wet with odorless, tasteless spermicidal jelly.

"Here." Chester hands her the camera and walks toward the sea lions; they're stretched out like a line of brown corpses, drowned and washed up after a shipping disaster, the ablating sea wearing away arms and legs and heads. He kneels next to a few. "Get me," he says.

"I'm not the home-movie auteur."

"Just do it."

"Okay, Mr. Nike." Debbie raises the camera and pushes the button to film. The view through the viewfinder—the blinking red REC in the corner—is the view that the robotic Debbie would see in this world, the robotic Debbie that would fool everybody, the robotic Debbie that would allow the real Debbie to remain unchanged. And maybe this robotic Debbie could be the happy wife, the happy mother with the babies, cyborg babies, their eyes Sharp, their ears Panasonic, their brains Microsoft.

"Are you getting good stuff?" Chester asks.

"I suppose."

"Here." Chester lies down on his stomach, the last in a row of sea lions baking in the sun. He closes his eyes. Debbie imagines a pissed-off beachmaster shambling toward her husband. A tragedy caught on tape. They've been known to attack, one time castrating a man who was swimming in the surf. She read that somewhere.

THIS is their third day of a five-day package deal. Chester booked the trip through FitzRoy Tours, a small outfit, a two-man operation: Miguel the Ecuadorian captain/cook/first mate and Edmund the British naturalist. The boat is a barely suitable cabin cruiser, recently converted from a twenty-five-foot fishing trawler. Miguel used to dive for sea cucumbers, popular in China and Japan, their slightly toxic juice thought to be an aphrodisiac, like a bear's liver or a rhino's horn, but more potent, almost hallucinogenic, a booming industry until the environmentalists came in and cried *Overharvesting!* and shut the whole thing down. The moment Chester saw the battered boat listing in the Puerto Ayora marina, he immediately understood the inexpensive package deal.

After consulting with the other naturalists, Edmund ambles over to Debbie. "Well," he says. Edmund enjoys preluding his sentences with a drawn-out interjection. Ah, fancy, goodness, ha, indeed, okay, ready now—those are some of his favorites. He has an educated accent, and he tells people he graduated Oxford, though the truth is an industrial university in a polluted city. "Don't know where we can go where it'll be less crowded. Um, this is the busy season."

"There must be someplace," Debbie says. "This is too many people."

"Alas, no, not if you want to see the animals of note."

"How about scuba diving?"

"Too many hammerhead sharks about."

"But your brochure said scuba diving."

"Oh, we can scuba dive, certainly, we have the proper equipment, yes, and Miguel is experienced, well, in his type of diving, you just have to watch out for the currents, and the sharks, of course, yes, you would have to sign a release. But we could do it if you like."

Chester lumbers to his feet and wipes sand from his knees. "What's up?" he says, coming over to the two of them. "Have we hit upon something?"

"Well, no," Edmund answers. "These islands are regulated to quite a degree, for tourists. So, as a result, space is crowded." Edmund crosses his arms, his hands feeling the material of his shirt. The naturalist wears khaki because it really is a cool material, lightweight and durable. Durable is important when you're slagging over lava, when you're slumming through cacti, when you're sashaying with women on the cruise ship, *The Princess Beagle,* stalking onto the Lido Deck and its cohabitating bar, The Origin of Cocktails. This place used to be one of Edmund's favorite haunts. A good watering hole. The staff from the ship, mostly young women, mostly Catholic, went there. And then there were the tourists, mostly couples and families—no fun—but sometimes single women, a group of girlfriends, older women, widows, students taking a school trip. That's what got him in trouble. Fired, really. Those fifteen-year-olds, the perfect age before the body begins storing fat for birthing, before the mind inhabits the perplexity of a point of view. They flaunted themselves in the kidney-shaped pool, not caring about wildlife, more concerned with their tans and their gossip, huddling in deck-chair packs. And Edmund would strut by, toss out a joke, always glad that the buttons of his shirt easily slipped from the buttonholes so that his chest was exposed by accident. One of them invariably fell in love.

"Edmund?"

"Ah, yes."

"I've had enough of sea lions." Debbie tosses down her

spent cigarette and heels it out in the sand. She waits a moment. Then she digs the butt out and holds it awkwardly as if the pleasant corruptibility of smoke is trumped by a surviving filter.

"Well, let's see." Edmund checks his watch. "We could have lunch back on the boat, then go to a different island, maybe one less popular."

Chester claps his hand. "Sounds good." He wants to be positive. It's simply not hard to be positive. Anything can be positive if you tweak the focus knob and play with the vertical hold and work on the tint.

Edmund leads the way toward the docking area, passing by pods of tourists listening to explanations in the language of their choice. Not too deep down, Edmund would rather be a great white hunter than a naturalist. It's a macho thing. He read Hemingway, he loved Clark Gable in *Sporting Blood*. But great white hunters are a dying breed and naturalists-for-rent are huge right now. It's fat stupid money, *Bos Moneta,* though sometimes the profession feels a bit faggy (try extolling the virtues of a blue-footed boobie with a straight face), and he would love to be able to sling a rifle over his shoulder and pursue some large animal. It's every naturalist's fantasy. Just ask one. To scope through a rifle instead of binoculars.

OUT IN the water, searching the water, trying to peer through the water to the depths below where sea cucumbers live, on the bottom, capturing nutrients or small aquatic animals in their retractile tentacles, Miguel waits in the *Zodiac* for Edmund and the clients. Today would be a good day for sea cucumbers. This thought constantly circulates in his head, even on days when it would be a bad day for sea cucumbers. To pass the time Miguel holds his breath and counts in his head to test his lung capacity. This skill is now a barroom trick, betting people he can last five minutes on a single toke of air. He always wins. But he misses the water and the burning in his chest and the search for the dull dark color of his trade.

Miguel glances up and sees Edmund frantically waving at him from the dock and shouting his name with bossy authority. Fuck him. Assholes like him are the ones who destroyed the cucumber fishery. Protect the species. What about the people? And now his boat is being used to serve their needs. What would his father say? *¿Puede darme unas cuchillas para afeitar?* But what can you do? You have to survive. Miguel pull-starts the outboard motor and skims the surface toward the landing. He wishes he had a family to support. That would've made the decision much easier. Young mouths to feed instead of his own.

"Well, it's about time," Edmund says.

"Dispénseme."

The three of them climb onto the *Zodiac*. Chester is the last on, and he stumbles a bit, almost going over the side. A funny guy, this giant, funny in a sad way. Reminds Miguel of Mestizo, the clown in the popular Brazilian TV show. All the kids in Guayaquil used to watch him, watched huge Mestizo get abused by neighbors, get lost going to the market, get chased by dogs, get shipwrecked on an island of cannibals. Each week Mestizo wallowed in some sort of misery, and it was just about the funniest thing you'd ever see. And the young studio audience would constantly shout out, "Ah, Mestizo, not again!" It was yelled in Portuguese, though adult actors, professional loopers, dubbed it into Spanish. This scared many of the boys in Ecuador because they assumed that the boys in Brazil were stronger, more developed, smarter, tougher, than the boys in Ecuador. Listen to their voices. So deep. So manly. And it all made sense when they watched the Brazilian footballers devastate the inadequate Ecuadorians.

Miguel starts cracking up, recalling the episode where

Mestizo falls into a pool of piranha. "Ah, Mestizo, not
again!" A chill prickles his skin.

Chester plops down on the inflated rubber bow. "Oops,"
he says, smiling at his clumsiness. "Don't quite have my sea
legs yet." He shuffles to the cross-plank where Debbie sits.
"Almost lost me there," he tells her.

She pats him on the knee.

Miguel throttles up and steers toward the ex-fishing boat
anchored in the cay.

LUNCH is make-your-own-sandwiches from a platter of lun-
cheon meats. They drink warm iced tea and sit on the deck
in canvas chairs, the sun hot, the islands in the distance
looking like the emerged backs of great prehistoric beasts.
There is silence, long silence, uncomfortable silence, until
Edmund says, "You know, Chester, there's a city of Chester
in Cheshire, my county. Still has its Roman walls. Only city
in England with its walls intact. Quite something, those
walls. Also quite something to see the Chester mystery plays,
the whole cycle, performed in Chester. Powerful. Christ rising in Chester. Yes, Chester. Something. You see, Chester
means 'camp.' In Latin. Castra to Ceaster to Chester. Also
British slang for 'molester.' A chester. A child chester. No one
wants to be chestered."

"What?"

"It's alliterative vernacular. No literary or historical rela-
tion. Not true with Peeping Tom. Or sadist with Sade."

"Okay."

"Bullshit."

"What?"

"Bullshit. I guess I said bullshit," admits Debbie.

Edmund smiles. "Well, T. S. Eliot coined that particular
usage."

"Huh?"

"You know, the poet. *The Waste Land*." The naturalist

rearranges himself in the chair so that his legs are in an intel-
lectual position: crossed tightly, with no wedge of space on his
lap, no acute-angled or obtuse-angled or right-angled triangle formed by a tacky intersection within the groin. Smart men
do it that way. Edmund knows this. On *The Princess Beagle*
he'd seen the rich tourists from California, Connecticut and
New York; been in the company of M.A.s and Ph.D.s, of
D.Phil.s and Ed.D.s and Litt.D.s; talked to two peers, three
blue bloods and a laird; almost had an affair with a sad
dame; once kissed a reinstated margravine; and was even
chestered by a drunken hidalgo. Within this list—and he
loves lists, a ladder of words that scroll within your skull, the
receipt ribbon of the intellect's cash register—Edmund is
positive that he's doing his Oxford heritage proud. He says,
"April's cruel and all that. Anyway, he came up with bullshit.
Or at least he's the first acknowledged user of the word."
    "Huh?"
    "B. S. Eliot, they called him."
    "What are you talking about?"
    "Eliot," Edmund is still saying, "wrote a poem called
Bullshit and the Ballad for Big Louise. It's a lost poem, I
believe. But Wyndham Lewis, around 1914, wrote a letter to
Ezra Pound talking about it, praising it. I guess it was filled
with quite a bit of ribaldry." Edmund knows the etymology
of vulgar terms, it's kind of his hobby, ever since he was a
boy and learned there was a realm of hidden words that por-
trayed hidden habits. He continues lecturing, happy to mer-
chandise his knowledge. "And ye old cunt and cock, the
grandmother and grandfather of profanity, they've been
around forever. A mix of Old English and Middle English to
create a bit of Low English." A pause for a chuckle. "With
cock you've got Field's *Amends for Ladies* with his, and I
quote, 'Oh man what art thou? when thy cock is up.' That's
circa 1250. Cunt's not much different. Well, I don't mean
that. They're quite different." A quick smile. "But date-wise

they're pretty close. Circa 1230. Elkwall's *Street Names of the City of London* has a Gropecuntelane. I shit you not, which is, by the way, a Dutch variant of the word 'shoot.' "

Chester checks Debbie's face. She doesn't seem offended, but still. "Excuse me, Edmund," he says, "I don't think that's appropriate."

"What's that?"

"Your language."

Debbie waves away the transgression. "No big deal. It's actually interesting."

Edmund nods. "Well, you have to be well-informed, I always say, informed about the words you might use, exact about it, no matter the word because what are words but the slow mutation of expression. I mean, how does a bad word become a bad word? How is it decided? When? Where does it turn from acceptable to unacceptable? When is the innocence lost? Huh?" Edmund waits for possible questions, then carries on. "My fascination with this matter was struck up when I confused etymology with entomology during my adolescent study of the dung beetle."

"You're fucking right," Debbie says.

"Ah, yes, the Scottish poet William Dunbar, in his elegy, around 1503, who wrote: 'Be hiis feiris he wuld have fukkit.' "

"What the fuck does that mean?"

"Not too sure, really. Middle English and all. Very difficult. The context, that is. How it was meant. Like take son of a bitch."

"A classic," says Debbie.

"Well, I once called my brother a son of a bitch, 'bitch' being a derivation of Old English *bicce* and Old Norse *bikkja*, as well as a form of my brother. I called him a son of a bitch because he called me a bastard, bastard from the eleventh-century Latin *bastardus, bastum, fils de bast.* Anyway, I didn't know what the phrase meant, I was only nine

years old, but my father heard what I had said, my father
who always liked my brother better, and he said, 'Shame on
you, calling your mum a bitch. Comparing Mum to a dog,
that what you meant?' 'No,' I said. 'Saying it to Edgar,' I
said. 'You fool,' he said, and he slapped me a hard one
against the cheek. 'Edgar called me a bastard,' I said, in
tears. And he said, 'Cause you are a bastard, you bastard.'
Smack. 'A whoreson but no son of a bitch.' Smack smack
smack. And then I had to go and apologize to my mother."
Edmund wipes his mouth. "Yep, bastard," he sighs. "Robert
of Gloucester is credited with the first usage. Around 1297.
'Of pulke blode Wyllam bastard com,' or something like
that." Edmund gets up, grabs some plates from the table,
and goes into the galley.

Debbie leans toward Chester. "Did we just hear that?"

"I think so."

She hums the theme to *The Twilight Zone*.

BEFORE cruising over to Santiago Island for an afternoon
hike, Edmund retires for a nap, and Miguel asks Chester and
Debbie if they want a local delicacy for dinner. "Something
special," he says in his broken English. "Maybe?"

The couple eye each other. "Sure," Debbie answers.

"Yeah, why not?" Chester seconds. "Sí."

A satisfied Miguel disappears belowdecks and soon
returns with a reticule in his hand and a diving mask tight on
his face. Smiling, he strips down to a pair of red Speedos, his
penis and testicles pressing against the fabric like a straw-
berry snout. He stands atop the rail and begins panting ten
deep breaths. His body rocks. Then he jumps overboard.

"Okay," Debbie says, watching the tranquil surface
reform from his splash.

Chester is next to her, almost touching her. "Abandon
ship."

"Not a bad idea."

"Sorry about this."

"Don't be."

Chester shrugs. "I don't think you're having a good time."

"I'm having a fine time. Don't worry." Debbie stares down into the water. It's very blue, almost unnaturally blue, as if dye had been spilled from some tanker on its way to Easter. She's surprised it doesn't leave a stain on the skin. "I wonder how deep it is?"

"I'd guess deep."

"What kind of delicacy lives down there?" she asks.

"Who knows? At least we know it's not albatross."

Debbie leans over the side and begins holding her breath but soon stops because it seems childish and spoiled. In the distance, frigate birds dive-bomb a beach for the newly hatched turtles paddling sand for faraway surf. A group of tourists stand in a semicircle, their bodies posed as if they're the people of Pompeii, preserved in lava, then dug up, then finally displayed in a natural setting.

"Jesus, how long has it been?"

"I don't know, a couple of minutes."

"Some lungs he must have."

Chester pats his left pocket and feels a brief panic at not feeling his house keys, that they are lost somewhere, then he remembers that they're in his duffel bag, hidden in an unused money belt with his wallet and passport and traveler's checks. He snorts at himself.

"What?" asks Deb.

"Nothing. Thought I'd been pickpocketed or something. Like this is Times Square or something."

"Give it time. All these people. Shoulder to shoulder."

"Well," Chester says, "we're here as well."

"True. Pangaea busted no more. Where is he?"

"Down there."

"Aquaman."

"Or a drowned man."

"How long has it been now?"

Chester check his watch. "About four minutes. Maybe."

"Should we worry, should we get Edmund?"

"That son of a bitch."

Debbie laughs. "That bastard."

"Maybe a shark got him."

"Or he's caught in kelp. I've seen that before. In a movie. Are you worried?"

Chester shakes his head. "Not yet. Not really." He cups his hands around his eyes. "Should I try to be a hero?"

"I don't know."

"Now is the summer of our discontent," says Chester.

"Where the hell did that come from?"

"I have no idea. I don't even know what it means." Chester kicks off his sandals. "Okay, maybe this is serious."

"You going in?" Debbie asks, her voice noncommittal.

"Uhm, probably not."

Then, about twenty yards from starboard-side, a shape surfaces, a bump in the blue, a hand waving, the glass of the mask glinting the sun like a Cyclopean monster. "Benito! Benito!" he cries, his breathy voice finding the long *h* in the pronunciation.

Chester and Debbie both say, "There he is," and they both point at the same time, codiscoverers of a new species of man.

Miguel swims to the boat, still crying, "Benito! Benito!"

"What does that mean?"

"Don't know."

"Is it good?"

Chester once again says, "I don't know."

Miguel grabs ahold of the ladder and climbs up onto the deck. Trailing behind him, in the reticule, is a large green thing, about a foot and a half long, as thick as a loaf of moldy bread, the skin plagued with warty growths. Miguel peels off his mask; a red oval remains behind, a dent of the pressure felt below. "Trepang," he says, digging his hands into the mesh and bringing out this underwater slug. He holds it forth like an offering. "Bêche-de-mer," he tells them.

Debbie says, "Wow," as if complementing a harelipped baby.

Chester nods his approval.

"Lick it," says Miguel, smiling, and just in case he hasn't been understood, he pantomimes the action.

"Lick it?"

"Sí. Lick." Miguel steps forward so that now the sea cucumber is right in front of them. On one end is a mossy beard of tentacles. "Special," he confides.

Chester makes a face of dissent. "I don't know about that. No. No," he says with a Spanish accent.

But Debbie wants to partake, seeing this mystery in front of her, this living creature that is not beautiful and not complex and not worthy to be loved by sightseers. Instead, it is part of the freak show of nature, kept in the tent where barkers dare you to proceed. The truly ugly are saved from the judgments of good or bad; only the deformed are free. Debbie leans forward, eyes closed, tongue out. She moves closer, waiting to make contact with the awfulness, and when she does, the skin waters her mouth. She runs her tongue along the soft bumpy exterior. A hint of salt, but mostly a tartness which tingles the taste buds and seems to open them to such a degree that they turn her mouth inside out en route to turning her whole body inside out. "Hmmmm," she says.

"What's it like, honey?"

She opens her eyes, the cucumber disfiguring her peripheral vision. She stares off to the side at Chester, at his wide face and his boxer's grin, at his dreams of family writ large in the sky above his head. Such a solid man. Dutiful and consistent. Understanding. Nowhere near the grotesque, but still lovely.

Miguel turns to Chester. "Try," he says. "Por favor."

Chester goes over to Debbie's side. "Here I come," he says, and he puts his arm around her waist and bends down, his tongue tensed and ready. But he stops. "What does this do?" he asks Miguel.

"You'll see."

"Nothing bad, right?"

"No. Benito, Mestizo. Benito, Mestizo."

"Okay." The spongy mass is throbbing, searching for the water in the air. Disgusting. An animated vegetable, crudités with a digestive tract, salad with teeth. But Chester begins sampling anyway, wanting to join his wife, to participate in the unknown, in the uncertain. He starts with just the tip of his tongue but soon he's lapping with the entire length of his median lingual sulcus.

"Mmmmm," Chester hums. And something rises in Debbie, a pheromonal phoneme in the "Mmmmm," a vibration and resonance that goes beyond the purely linguistic and pokes into prosody, a meaning, a connection, a rhythmic impulse for its own ends. A human art. It's like her husband is Rock Hudson—a thing, a place, a person.

When one side is finished, Miguel turns the sea cucumber like a father feeding his children.

IN HIS bunk, the air heavy with funky heat, Edmund dreams not the dream about his family—that's the bad dream—but the dream about the fifteen-year-old girls, the good dream, where he is guiding Clarissa or Meaghan or Vanessa or Stacey or Penny to his cabin on *The Princess Beagle,* and they are holding hands, his index finger hooked within her rope bracelet, her shoulder bumping against his shoulder in charged incidental contact, and she is slightly drunk from illicit Tequila Sunrises and nicely scented from overenthused disco dancing, while he's hoping that his erection isn't protuberating khaki; they stop in front of his door; he digs for

keys; she slumps against the wall . . . Edmund normally wakes up at this moment, wakes up before he gets into his cabin, and when he wakes up he usually has a concrete hard-on. Oftentimes, like right now, he'll quickly masturbate so as to relieve this lingering memory, stroking himself, continuing the abbreviated dream: the waltz to the bed, the undressing, the thrill of seeing a naked body for the first time, the tits, the pussy—those words, animal-related, now turned into adolescent slang. And as he imagines tan lines he hears a noise on the other side of the wall, a moaning male and female, speaking muffled phrases of "Fuck my cunt" and "Suck my cock," classic porno dialogue, and Edmund wonders if he might still be dreaming, if in the next room he's finally making love with one of these schoolgirls, finishing the dream yet not able to participate, hearing what sounds like frantic birds caught in a room, banging walls, dashing their brains in search of the passage that brought them here, the wood hollering as if it cannot hold much longer, as if every second might be the last second before whatever it is comes rushing through.

Acknowledgments

Much thanks to Gillian Blake, Alexa Brandenberg, Bill Clegg, Charis Conn, Rhian Ellis, Nan Graham, Andy Greer, Mark Holthoff, Charlie Howard, John Lennon, Cressida Leyshon, Jeff Odefey, Kathy Robbins, Ed Skoog, and especially Susie Leness.